JACK BE NIMBLE

ADAM CROFT

GET MORE OF MY BOOKS FREE!

To say thank you for buying this book, I'd like to invite you to my exclusive *VIP Club*, and give you some of my books and short stories for FREE.

To join the club, head to adamcroft.net/vip-club **and two free books will be sent to you straight away! And the best thing is it won't cost you a penny —** ever.

Adam Croft

For more information, visit my website: adamcroft.net

BOOKS IN THIS SERIES

Books in the Knight and Culverhouse series so far:

1. Too Close for Comfort
2. Guilty as Sin
3. Jack Be Nimble

To find out more about this series and others, please head to adamcroft.net/list.

31ST AUGUST

It felt odd punching an unconscious woman. Wrong, almost. Almost. The tranquilliser wouldn't be wearing off for some time yet, so he had plenty of time to revel in the rollercoaster of emotions.

He steadied himself by leaning forward on the edge of the bathtub, the plastic wrap crunching and rustling as he did so. He had a sudden urge to spit in her face, but knew he had to control himself. Leaving his DNA on the body wouldn't be a great start.

It was getting almost unbearably hot inside the beekeeper's suit but he couldn't remove anything until it was all over. It just wasn't worth the risk.

He pulled the knife out of its leather sheath and turned it in his hand, the light glistening off the steel and bouncing around the room. He pulled it under his nostrils and sniffed. It smelt of nothing — perhaps faintly of leather — but it wasn't the smell he was interested in. It was the sensation.

He looked down at her body and noticed a red mark already appearing where he'd punched her. All he needed to do now was wait until a bruise had started to develop. He couldn't kill her before then, as much as he desperately wanted to. He was fighting the urge with every fibre of his being. He didn't know whether it was excitement, joy or extreme anxiety. Right now he knew only one thing: he had to stick to the plan.

Going off track now could be disastrous. Every minuscule aspect of this had to be carried out to a T. For every stage, he'd even worked out a secondary and, in most cases, a tertiary option should unforeseen circumstances arise. Because unforeseen circumstances always arose.

The only thing he could not be sure of were the exact timings, but that didn't matter too much. The plan he was working from didn't have exact timings. He knew that the red mark on her face would build slightly and some swelling would occur. With any luck, he'd have cracked her cheekbone or caused tissue damage which would be spotted anyway. He wasn't waiting for a full-on purple shiner — that could take days. No, just a nice red welt would do. Enough for them to spot it.

Cutting through her neck hadn't felt at all like he had expected it to. It was like slicing a tough, stringy chicken breast. Even with his ultra-sharp knife he had to rock the knife and work with it to get the effect he wanted. Before long he was almost down to the vertebrae. He'd placed a plastic screen over her upper body and was now struggling to see through it, such was the amount of blood that'd hit it. This job needed to be clean, though, because they couldn't catch him. Not just yet. Not until he was ready.

He carefully peeled back the plastic glove over his left wrist to look at his watch. It was almost time.

2

DCI Jack Culverhouse stood ashen-faced at his front door, staring out at the figure in front of him. He wasn't used to having late-night callers, and he certainly wasn't expecting this one.

'Hello Jack,' she said as she tried to force a smile.

For him, though, no words were forthcoming. The last time he'd seen Helen was eight and a half years ago, the day she'd walked out and taken their three-year-old daughter Emily with her. That day seemed as though it could have been a century ago, but at the same time, seeing her face before him again now, it felt like it was only yesterday.

Her hair was shorter, cut neatly and shaped around the jawline, with fading highlights which had evidently been put in a few months ago. She'd still kept her slim figure, Jack noticed. At least that was something.

'You probably weren't expecting to see me,' she said as she pushed a straight lock of hair behind her ear.

'No. I can't say I was.'

'Can I come in?' she asked, tilting her head slightly to one side.

This wasn't exactly a situation which had certain protocol or etiquette attached to it. Not that Jack Culverhouse was a man for protocol or etiquette. For eight and a half years he'd imagined this moment, thought about what he'd say if it ever happened. What could he possibly say? After eight and a half years, he still didn't have an answer to that question.

Part of him — an ever-decreasing part — was pleased to see her. She was, after all, his wife. The anger and resentment had also subsided over the years. For the first year or two, he would've slammed the door in her face, no questions asked. But now those feelings had waned and he found himself feeling absolutely no emotion for a woman he'd married and fathered a child with.

His feelings for Emily had certainly not diminished, though. A father's love never fades.

All of this flashed through his mind in a split-second before he answered the only way he knew how.

'I don't see why not.'

The first thought that crossed his mind as he closed the front door was how strange it was that Helen had had to ask to enter what was, essentially, her own house. He'd never got round to removing her name from the deeds. He'd need her permission to do that anyway, and he had no way of getting in contact with her. At least, that was his justification for not doing it.

Managing the mortgage on his own hadn't been a problem. He'd been doing that anyway, before she left, but afterwards he'd had the added bonus of not having to clear her credit card bill each month too.

'I suppose you want to know why I'm here,' she said as she sat down on the sofa and leant forward, her elbows on her knees.

'No, I just thought we could have a cup of tea and play happy fucking families again.'

Helen smiled. 'Still got your acerbic wit, I see.'

'Is that what it is?' Culverhouse replied. 'Personally, I call it realism.'

'You can sit down, you know.'

Culverhouse raised his eyebrows. 'What, in my own house? How very kind of you.'

Helen's smile faded. 'Sit down, Jack.'

Culverhouse did as he was told.

'I really don't know where to start,' she said, staring at her feet. 'I've been planning this for so long, how to explain and get it to make sense for you. It doesn't really make much sense to me, if I'm honest, but there we go. It's not really something you can ever explain, is it? I mean, how do you find the right words to say—'

'Where have you been?' Culverhouse interrupted, more as a statement than a question.

'Spain.'

'Oh, lovely. At least you were sunning yourself and enjoying sangria and siestas, then.'

'It's not all that,' she said, looking back at her feet.

'And what about Emily?' he asked, his voice lowered.

'She's fine.'

'Where is she?'

'She's not here,' Helen answered.

'Well I can bloody well see that,' Culverhouse replied,

standing and pacing towards the kitchen with his hands thrust in his pockets.

'She didn't want to come. And before you say it, yes, I did try and get her to. But she didn't want to. You have to understand, Jack, she barely knows you.'

'Of course she doesn't! You took her away when she was three years old, Helen. What do you think that does to a kid?'

Helen remained silent.

'Where is she? Who's she with?' he asked.

Helen sighed. 'She's with David.'

'David? Who's David?'

'He's my partner.'

Culverhouse nodded slowly. 'I see. And does she call him Daddy?' It sounded ridiculous, but it was the first thing he could think to say.

'No, of course she doesn't,' came the reply. In all his years of police training and experience, he could still never tell whether or not his wife was telling the truth. 'What about you, Jack? Haven't you moved on? It's been eight and a half years.'

Culverhouse let out a small snort before he spoke. 'I know exactly how long it's been, Helen. And no, I haven't. I'm married. To you.'

'Only legally,' Helen replied in a small voice. 'Never emotionally. Emotionally, you were always married to the job. I can see some things never change,' she said, pointing to the Mildenheath CID lanyard hanging around his neck. 'I mean, am I being interviewed or are we having a chat? It's gone midnight, for Christ's sake.'

Culverhouse looked at the lanyard and took it off, throwing it on top of the lounge sideboard.

'It meant nothing to you back then and it'll probably mean

nothing now, but it's not a nine to five job, Helen. It's a way of life. A way of life you bought into.'

'Yes, yes, I know. But do you have any idea what it was like to have to try and bring up a child, pretty much on my own? Do you think I just wanted to use you for the free roof over my head and the occasional bonk when you'd got home at three in the morning? That's not a marriage, Jack. We both deserved better than that.'

'So why didn't we ever talk about it?' he replied. 'Why just up and leave? What did that solve?'

'I don't know. I still don't know. It just seemed like the right thing to do. I know that sounds crazy, but it's true.'

Culverhouse looked at his wife as she sat staring at the carpet and wondered if he'd ever really known her at all.

3

Even though it was gone midnight, DS Wendy Knight was still wide awake. She'd not really enjoyed a full night's sleep in a long time. Being a Detective Sergeant attached to the local murder squad wasn't exactly conducive to a peaceful slumber at the best of times, but recent times had been particularly unkind to Wendy.

Her first serial killer case had not only led to her having to try and clear the name of her then lover, Robert, but also the stark realisation that the murderer had been closer to home than she'd realised.

Get back on the horse, her father had always told her. Bill Knight had been a CID officer himself, and those words of his had echoed around Wendy's mind in the days and weeks following the closure of her first serial killer case.

Getting back on the horse had been relatively easy. It was falling off again that hurt. First came the discovery that she was pregnant with her dead partner's baby before suffering a miscarriage after a foot chase with a petty criminal. And all whilst trying to solve a double murder case just weeks after the first.

Sleep hadn't been the first thing on Wendy's mind for a long time. Neither had unpacking her belongings and making her new house a home. The house wasn't strictly new any more — she'd been here a while — but the plethora of cardboard boxes scattered around had kept the illusion alive for longer than usual.

She'd tried to justify her lack of diligence in unpacking on some vague notion that she might decorate a couple of the rooms before long. Deep down, she knew that would never happen and had now resolved to finally stop living out of cardboard boxes.

The kitchen was now almost complete. At least now she'd be able to cook for herself rather than relying on ready meals and takeaways. She'd privately scolded herself for unpacking the microwave before anything else on the day she'd moved in.

Tearing off the parcel tape from one box marked *General nicknacks*, she paused as she opened the cardboard flaps and saw, sitting at the top, a framed photograph of her and Michael in happier times. The photo had been taken a year or two after their father had died, but whilst their mother was still alive. As Wendy picked the photo up she felt strangely as though she were her mother, who'd taken the photo and stood seeing this exact same image at the moment it was taken. The mother who'd felt that exact same antithesis of motherly protection over him and shame at what he'd become.

Michael's drug addiction had spiralled since his first forays into experimenting with ecstasy in local nightclubs when he was eighteen. It was clear to both Wendy and her mother that Michael was missing a certain love for life which he was replacing with substances, inevitably resulting in his moving on to heroin and crack cocaine, both of which became dangerous addictions.

He'd tried to kick the habit a number of times, and had succeeded for short periods of time, but Michael was the sort of addict who'd unfortunately always be an addict for one simple reason: he didn't want to help himself. He'd seen himself as a hopeless cause and had been unable to break the self-fulfilling spiral of depression and substance abuse.

What had turned him to do what he did, though, was still a mystery to Wendy. She knew from her experience as a police officer that doing what he'd done and being a drug addict were far from being connected, but part of her had always wondered whether it had caused some sort of chemical alteration in his brain.

Those long nights when she'd been unable to sleep had often been taken up with her own analyses of what had happened, what had gone wrong. Had there been something lacking in Michael from an early age? Could she recall anything which might have been an early sign that he was going to go on to do what he did? There was nothing that sprung to mind, but then again what would? She knew there was no such thing as the Hollywood early warning sign; no general tendency for would-be evildoers to practise their murderous urges on frogs or mice.

No matter how many nights she lay awake trying to think of one, she could think of no particular event which could have led Michael down that path, which led her to only one worrying conclusion: that it was something inbuilt. And that, alone, worried her. After all, he was her brother. They were genetically similar.

Genetically speaking, Michael was half Bill Knight, the

much-admired and much-missed legendary murder detective and half Sue Knight, the dearly missed town councillor and mother who'd done so much for her family and local community. Genetically speaking, he should have been the perfect human being. But something had gone very, very wrong.

The lack of answers and closure had played on Wendy's mind ever since, but it had had one satisfying resolution: that she was determined to ensure it was the legacies of her parents that lived on; not her brother's.

4

Eight and a half years did a lot to a person. It had certainly done a lot to Jack Culverhouse, and he could see it had done a lot to Helen. In many ways she was still the same person he'd known so well, but he could also see the effect life had had on her. In many ways, it had been cruel.

'Just tell me one thing,' he said as he leant back in the armchair and rubbed his brow with his thumb and forefinger, having spent the last couple of hours enduring baseless small talk. 'What did you say to Emily?'

'When?' Helen asked, looking up at him.

'When you went away. And after. Since then.'

'Nothing,' she replied, not sounding altogether convincing.

'Don't lie to me, Helen. It's my job to know when people are lying.'

Helen made a derisive snort and looked away. 'And there it goes again. The job.'

'Don't change the subject,' he said, leaning forward in the chair. 'I don't believe for a second that she wouldn't want to see me. I'm her dad.'

'She doesn't remember you, Jack. She was three years old.'

Culverhouse jumped to his feet and walked over to the window. 'It doesn't matter if she remembers me. That's not the point. Any kid would want to see their dad if they hadn't seen him for eight and a half years. Unless they'd been told some bullshit about him and made to believe he was some kind of animal.' He looked at Helen as he said this and thought he detected an almost imperceptible reaction in her eyes. 'That's it, isn't it? You've fed her some story to stop her wanting to come back. What is it? What did you tell her?' he asked, his voice having now risen almost to the level of shouting.

'I didn't need to tell her anything, Jack. You managed to do that all yourself. She might only have been three years old but kids pick things up at that age. Look at you, stood there trying to intimidate me. Is it any wonder she doesn't want to see you?'

'That's fucking bullshit, Helen and you know it,' he replied, getting angrier as he spoke. 'Yes, I'm shouting at you and yes I'm fucking angry but you made me like this. Don't ever try to say I was like this back then, because I wasn't. Yes, I was dedicated to my job — and I still am — but I was happy. I was positive. I was calm. I wasn't an angry person back then and you know it.'

Helen smirked. 'What, so it's my fault now is it?'

'I never asked you to leave, Helen. I didn't even know there was a problem until I came home that night and found your letter.'

Helen stood and rose to meet his eye. 'And if you had known, would you have done anything about it? Would you have changed?'

Culverhouse was silent for a moment longer than Helen might have liked. 'I would've tried.'

'Tried? Oh yes, you always tried. But trying's not always

good enough, Jack. You know, I thought I was mad coming back here. I hoped we might be able to get along like adults and get to the point where Emily would want to see you and we could have some sort of normality. I can see that's not going to happen. I don't know why I wasted my time.' As she bent down to pick up her handbag and leave, Culverhouse grabbed her arm as if to stop her going, knocking the handbag out of her hand as the two of them watched the small cardboard packet fall out and land on the carpet. He bent down to pick it up.

'Aripiprazole,' he said, reading the packet. 'What is it?'

Helen grabbed the packet from him and stuffed it back into her bag. 'It's nothing, don't worry about it.'

He put an arm on her shoulder and guided her to sit back down. 'It's obviously not nothing. Tell me, Helen. What's it for?'

Helen remained silent for a few moments before letting out a huge sigh. 'It's for helping me cope.'

'Cope? With what?'

'With life. It helps stabilise my moods and stop me doing daft, compulsive things and upsetting people.'

Culverhouse rubbed his brow. 'What do you mean? Is it like depression or a mental breakdown or something?'

'No, not really,' she replied, before realising that he was still none the wiser. 'It's a crossover of Cluster B personality disorders, they think mostly BPD and HPD but with elements of ASPD.'

Culverhouse looked at his wife. 'You know I don't have a fucking clue what you're on about, right?'

'I'm a nut job, Jack. I don't think properly and I hurt people.'

'Christ. They give you drugs for that now? Maybe I should get myself a prescription.'

'It's not a joke,' she said, making eye contact with him. 'I had... an episode. An incident. I spoke to doctors and they started me on some treatment programmes. This is why I wanted to come and see you. To help make amends for the past and to deal with my issues.'

Culverhouse just nodded, trying to understand but failing.

'Look, it's best that I go now. We can catch up at a better time. I'm here for a little while yet,' she said, scribbling a mobile phone number down on a scrap of paper in her bag. 'This is my UK mobile. Give me a call tomorrow and we'll sort something out properly.'

'Right. So we're just leaving it like that, are we?' Culverhouse said, pocketing the piece of paper.

'I think it's best we both get some sleep,' came the reply.

'Sleep? Oh yeah, I'll nod off nicely after all this,' Culverhouse said. 'Put my mind right at rest, this has.'

'What do you want to know?' Helen asked, sitting back down on the edge of the sofa.

'Well, everything. But for now, this personality thing. The disorder. What... What does it do?'

'I'm not about to flip out and kill you if that's what you mean,' she replied, smiling. 'I don't know if it's something that has always been there or if it's developed. It definitely started to get worse around the time I left. It was like some sort of uncontrollable impulse. I had to go. I had to. It just overrode everything else. I had no thought for what it would do to you or Emily or to anyone else. Looking back now, it seems mad. But hindsight's biggest downfall is that it's always too late, isn't it?'

'I guess so,' Culverhouse replied, finally feeling as though he had her in a position where she felt comfortable to talk. This was progress, he told himself. 'What did you do, though? What did you say? I mean, Emily was only young at the time but you must've had to explain it to her at some point since.'

'I don't remember.'

'You know, your friends wouldn't speak to me after. I remember one day I was in town and I saw that girl Janice you used to work with. She'd just crossed the road with a double buggy and as soon as she saw me she crossed straight back over again. She looked right at me and it was like she'd seen a ghost.' Culverhouse looked at his wife as if willing her to explain. 'Why would she do that?'

'I don't know,' Helen said. 'She'd always been a bit odd.'

'Tell me the truth, Helen. We're both being open and honest now.'

'I don't know what you mean. I didn't say a word.'

Culverhouse could feel the blood pulsing in his veins as he got angrier. 'Helen, I'm a police officer. I know when people are lying and holding things back. And I know damn well when people have been told things that aren't true. Like your friends. And Emily. You spun them a web of lies about me and now you can't find your way out of it. Am I right or am I right?' he barked, now inches from her face.

She stood up. 'Alright, yes. I did. I told them all you were a fucking monster. And do you know what? It looks like I was right.' She picked up her bag and marched towards the front door before he could stop her, only pausing once she had her hand on the latch. 'You know what? I felt really shitty about what I'd done. I admit, I was wrong about you before. Perhaps I shouldn't have said those things. But after seeing how you've changed, I feel vindicated. You know that monster I invented? You've become him, Jack.'

The door slammed in front of him as his wife walked out

again. At least this time he had something approaching an explanation.

He walked into his kitchen and tried to make sense of what had just happened over the past couple of hours. As he tried to piece everything together, his mobile phone vibrated in his pocket; a long, repeating pattern which told him he had an incoming call. He pulled it out and jabbed the answer button.

'Culverhouse.'

Once again, work had got in the way.

5

Albert Road was in the Victorian part of Mildenheath, amongst a collection of similar-looking streets constructed in the mid to late 1800s. The houses were mostly terraced, and parking was always an issue as accounting for two-car families had naturally not been an issue at the forefront of most Victorian architects' minds. This, Culverhouse was finding out as he tried to find somewhere to leave his car in the early hours of that morning. In the end, he opted for the middle of the street, noting that the uniformed officers were closing off both ends shortly after he'd arrived anyway.

The alleyway through to George Street was almost all that broke up the monotony of terraced housing and it was in this alleyway that the body had been found. A uniformed officer greeted Culverhouse as the officer in charge and briefed him on what had been discovered.

'It's a woman, no identity at the moment but we're working on that. Looks like the cause of death was a severe laceration to the side of her neck. It's gone right down to the bone, by the look of things. Only thing is, there's very little blood at the scene so it doesn't look like she died there. Looks more like a dumping ground to me.'

'I see,' Culverhouse said, his earlier interaction with Helen having worn him out mentally. On any other day, he'd have made a comment to the young officer as he wasn't keen on having what he saw as vague theories clouding his early judgement of a murder scene. As he approached the body, he recognised the familiar figure of Dr Janet Grey unpacking her box of tricks a few feet away.

'We meet again,' Culverhouse said as he reached her.

'Indeed we do. And yet again it's over a stiff. I'm starting to think you're bad luck, Jack.'

Culverhouse let out a small chuckle. 'I did apply to join the Fluffy Bunnies and Rainbows Division but they wouldn't have me.'

'Don't blame them,' Dr Grey replied, pulling on a rubber glove and snapping it against her wrist.

'Any first impressions?' Culverhouse asked, nodding to the body. Janet Grey was someone whose opinion he greatly valued, mainly because she was usually right.

'Well, she's definitely dead,' Dr Grey said, smiling. 'Judging by the wound on her neck and the fact that there's practically no blood here, my only other presumption at the moment would be that she was killed somewhere else and dumped here.'

Culverhouse heard the satisfied chuckle from behind him and spun round to find the young officer stood only a few feet away. The look Culverhouse shot him soon wiped the smile off his face and he walked back off towards the police cordon.

'Weird dumping ground, though,' Dr Grey continued. 'Usually when that happens the killer either hides the body away somewhere so no-one finds it or they leave it right out in the open so it's discovered quickly and sends a message. This one's odd. It's kind of a halfway house.'

'What about the injuries?' Culverhouse asked.

'Again, odd. Huge incision on the side of her neck, right down to the vertebrae. That'd leave a hell of a lot of blood, but her clothes seem pretty neat. They're bloody, but I'd expect them to be absolutely covered. Slash marks to the abdomen, too. Difficult to say in this light, but looks like they were done from left to right. Oh, and the bruising to her cheek. Looks like she was punched in the face. Not sure that would have knocked her unconscious, though. Almost certainly not for long enough for our killer to have been able to mutilate her in this way.'

'Any early instincts on what happened then?' Culverhouse pretended to itch the underside of his nose, but in reality he was trying to mask his senses from the smell that was now starting to emanate from the dead body.

'Difficult to say. Doesn't look as though she's been hacked at, though. In fact, it's pretty precise work. Almost surgical. Whoever did it seemed to know where the major arteries were so she'd bleed out quickly. The abdominal lacerations seem a little more emotionally led but still quite considered. It's the choice of dumping ground that concerns me, though. If she was killed somewhere else, then there's a hell of a lot of blood lying around somewhere.'

What worried Culverhouse was that the site where the dead body lay was barely four hundred yards from Mildenheath Police Station, which sat directly opposite the far end of Albert Street. Not only that, but this was a densely populated area of town and, even at this ungodly hour, transporting and leaving a dead body here would've been a risky business to say the least.

Murder could usually be split into two distinct types: a rush of blood to the head in which one person kills another on the spot and the premeditated, planned type. If it was an unplanned, unexpected killing, there'd be far more to go on. The fact that the body had been moved and then left more or less in the open was what worried Culverhouse. That showed some level of forethought and planning. Leaving it out on display was the mark of an unplanned murder, but this body had been moved to this location. So why not go the whole hog and try to dispose of the body permanently? Why move it to a more visible location? It reeked of someone trying to send a message, but Culverhouse didn't yet know who was sending the message, who they were sending it to or what the message was.

Crimes of passion and fights gone wrong were much easier to investigate. An impulsive killing would undoubtedly leave clues and quite possibly even witnesses, but a planned, premeditated murder was always far more daunting. Although he had very little to go on at this early stage, it seemed to DCI Jack Culverhouse as though this particular murder had been thought through very carefully indeed.

The incident room at Mildenheath CID was buzzing that morning. Serious crime was not only a growing part of everyday life in Mildenheath, but for the CID officers murder had been becoming more commonplace. Even so, the discovery of a body and the opening of a new case could still produce a frisson of excitement.

Culverhouse had assembled the same team that had assisted him in previous cases, choosing to reward loyalty as he was wont to do. Detective Sergeant Wendy Knight was to be his second in command, with Detective Sergeants Frank Vine, Steve Wing and Luke Baxter providing assistance.

Wendy was not Luke Baxter's biggest fan. Like most of the rest of the officers in CID, she had worked her way up from the bottom and earned her position as a Detective Sergeant. Her father had been a CID officer and the world of policing had always been a way of life for her. Baxter, on the other hand, had joined the police force fresh out of university and was being fast-tracked through the ranks with the support, if not the impetus, of DCI Culverhouse. She wasn't opposed to people progressing in their careers, but cocky wet-behind-the-ears people like Baxter really got on her nerves.

As was usual, Culverhouse had asked everyone to be ready for a nine o'clock briefing yet was the last person to arrive, just before quarter past.

'Right,' he said as he strode through the door and dumped a manila file on his desk. 'First things first, I've been up all night hanging around in alleyways with Dr Grey, so I'm not in the mood for any pratting about, which includes,' he added, looking directly at a chuckling Frank Vine, 'sniggering about what I just said. We have a victim, female, probably mid to late forties. No identity as of yet.' As he spoke, Culverhouse removed some printed photos of the crime scene and pinned them to the board behind him. 'Dr Grey says the victim died elsewhere and was dumped at the location by the killer. Why, we don't know. My first priority was to get onto the local press to announce that a body had been found and to try and find out who our victim was. It's just gone out on the hourly news bulletin on local radio, so hopefully we'll have a lead at some point soon.'

'I'll get onto Missing Persons as well, guv. See if I can match anything up there,' DC Debbie Weston said.

'No need. I've already done it,' said Luke Baxter. 'Nothing on record that seems to fit.'

'Right. Thank you,' Debbie said, nodding. Culverhouse had, in years gone by, tried to urge DC Weston to apply for a promotion but she had always been perfectly happy to remain a Detective Constable. Secretly, he'd been quite happy as it meant his Major Incident team could remain together, albeit a little DS-heavy.

Other Major Incident teams were usually more balanced in terms of the ranks of officers involved, but with Mildenheath having only the one CID team, it was seen as something of a law unto itself at county level. There had been whispers that Mildenheath CID would be brought under the auspices of an all-encompassing county-level CID department — as had all other satellite squads in the county — and there were even rumours of a pan-county CID setup being touted, meaning that their local independence would be truly lost. For now, though, Mildenheath CID was an odd, outdated quirk of plain clothes policing and that suited Jack Culverhouse just fine.

'In the meantime,' Culverhouse said, 'We'll need to do some door-to-door work in the Albert Street area to find out if anyone saw or heard anything. Can't be easy to sneak a dead body into an alleyway around there, even at that time of night. Debbie and Frank, can you get onto that? Luke, I'll need you to find out what CCTV coverage there is in the area. There's got to be someone with a camera on their house, or a nearby shop that'll have picked something up.'

Wendy looked at Culverhouse and noted that there was something different — more muted — about him. His opening warning aside, he'd seemed rather more subdued than usual. If it was anyone else, she would've put this down to him having been up all night, but she knew Jack Culverhouse and that should've only made him worse.

'The description that's been circulated is that of a woman aged in her forties, with shoulder-length mousey brown hair, wearing a purple strapped top and blue denim jeans. She had a silver ring on her right hand in the shape of a heart.' As he read the description, Culverhouse handed out sheets of paper with it written on, alongside details of where the body was found and at what time. For now, this was the only point of reference the team would have with which to begin the investigation.

'Was there no jacket or coat?' Wendy asked.

'Not at the scene,' Culverhouse replied. 'I know what you're thinking. Cold night, early hours, not exactly going to want to go out without a coat. But then again we don't know she was outside. If she was killed elsewhere, it could have been anywhere. More than likely indoors. Debbie and Frank, the door-to-door enquiries'll need to cover that. See if anyone remembers a woman fitting our victim's description entering a property nearby at any point in the last day or so.'

Before they could answer, there was a knock at the door and a young uniformed sergeant entered the room to let Culverhouse know he'd just received a phone call and needed to tell him about it. Culverhouse handed over to Wendy and stepped out of the room.

'Well, I think that's most of it covered actually,' Wendy said. 'Unless anyone has anything they'd like to raise?'

'Yeah. I shouldn't think it'd be a local house that she went into, if any,' Frank Vine said. 'Would be a bit risky, considering how close together the houses are. You wouldn't want to dump the body too close to home, would you?'

'True,' Wendy replied, 'but the further our killer had to take the body, the higher the risk of him being seen doing it. I don't think logic comes into it too much, either. That alleyway isn't a logical place to leave a body, especially if the victim wasn't killed there. I think it's safe to say our first priority needs to be identifying the victim. Once we know who our body is, finding the killer will be a whole lot easier.'

'On which note,' Culverhouse said, barging through the door back into the incident room, 'you'll be pleased to know that our radio appeal might have had some success. We've just had a call from a bloke who reckons our body sounds just like his ex-wife.'

7

Culverhouse had considered the call to be important enough for him to make the visit to Keira Quinn's ex-husband himself, taking Wendy along with him. Wendy wasn't sure what information he'd been passed, but knowing that Culverhouse was usually skeptical about random callers she assumed it must have been something of note.

They pulled up outside number 42 Parkview Road, part of an estate built at the foot of Mildenheath Common.

'Nice view,' Wendy said, gesturing towards the Common.

'Yeah, well you'd need it living round here, wouldn't you,' Culverhouse replied. The Parkview Road area wasn't the worst area of Mildenheath by any stretch of the imagination, but she had to admit that it wasn't exactly Meadow Hill Lane.

The man who answered the door was smartly dressed in a blue striped shirt tucked into dark trousers, the sun glistening off his belt buckle as he stepped aside to let them in.

'Thank you for your time, Mr Quinn,' Culverhouse said as he sat down on the sofa in the living room.

'Andy,' the man said before Culverhouse could continue.

'You spoke to my colleague on the phone earlier and said you had reason to believe the body found off Albert Road might have been that of your ex-wife.'

'Yeah, that's right,' Andy Quinn replied. 'The description sounded just like her. The top — she's had it for years. And when I heard about the heart-shaped ring on her right hand, I just stopped dead in my tracks. I think... I think that might be a ring I gave her years ago.'

'Would she still be wearing it?' Culverhouse asked, an eyebrow raised.

'Oh yeah, definitely. She's a sentimental sort of person,' Quinn replied, perching on the arm of a chair and wringing his hands. 'She's not the sort of person to let go very easily. I should know. Our relationship was well past its sell-by date.'

'Did she have any other distinguishing features?' Culverhouse asked, glancing around the room, trying to take in as much as he could.

'Not that I can think of,' Quinn said after a few seconds' silence. 'No tattoos or anything like that.'

'Birthmarks?'

'No. I don't think so.'

'Do you have any pictures of your wife?' Wendy asked.

'I don't, no. We got divorced and I didn't really see any sense in keeping photos of her about the house. Sorry.'

Culverhouse nodded. He could certainly sympathise with him there, although he did feel it was perhaps a little pointless having come out to Andy Quinn's house when they could now only rely on him identifying the body. 'How long have you been divorced?'

'Officially, about three years,' Quinn replied. 'We must've broken up a hundred times before that, though. Just one of those relationships which was doomed from the start. Poison, y'know. Better off without each other.'

'Any kids?' Culverhouse asked.

'No, thank God. It was messy enough as it was, without that.'

Before Culverhouse could respond, his mobile phone started to ring. He excused himself and went into the hallway to answer it.

Wendy glanced around the room and noticed a distinct lack of photos of any sort. 'Do you live here alone?' she asked.

Quinn paused for a moment longer than Wendy would've liked. 'No, my partner stays here most nights. She's away for work a lot, but she bases herself here.'

'Partner?' she asked.

'Yes, Erin. We've been together a year or so.'

'And did you still see Keira at all?'

'No, not really. She kind of... Well, she went off the rails a bit after we broke up. We don't exactly move in the same circles any more.'

Wendy was going to ask him to elaborate, but was interrupted by Culverhouse coming back into the room.

'That was Frank,' he said. 'They've been to your ex-wife's address and can't get any answer, so I'm afraid we'll need you to come and identify the body.'

Wendy watched Quinn closely, looking for any sign of emotion in his eyes, but she saw none.

The mortuary technician, Robyn Heslop, smiled in that neutral yet reassuring way that only people well acquainted with grieving families can manage. Andy Quinn stood silently in the doorway, as if about to take a step into a lion's den.

'You only need to tell us if this is your ex-wife, Keira, Andy,' Wendy said, having elected to take the lead in this sensitive situation rather than leave it to Culverhouse.

'You should be prepared for her to look a bit different,' Robyn Heslop added, her hand hovering over the corner of the sheeting that covered the body. 'She has some injuries to her face.'

Andy Quinn made a small choking noise, almost as if he was holding back a sob, and nodded. Robyn Heslop pulled back the sheeting.

Having already seen images of Keira Quinn's body, and not being overly keen to see it in the flesh, Wendy instead opted to keep her eyes fixed on Keira's ex-husband. His furrowed brow relaxed slightly as the recognition flashed across his face.

'Yes,' he whispered. 'That's her. That's Keira.'

8

Wendy volunteered to drive back to the station, the pair having taken Andy Quinn home again. She found that driving helped her to process her thoughts, and she had plenty of those going through her head today.

'I mean, it's pretty normal to expect a different reaction to an ex-wife dying than your present wife, but didn't he strike you as a bit odd?' Wendy asked a quiet Culverhouse as she slowed down for yet another red traffic light. 'And before you say it, yes I know, people grieve in different ways. But he seemed almost... Not pleased, but peaceful. Yeah, peaceful. Didn't you think?'

She glanced sideways at Culverhouse. He was nodding acquiescently in the way he always did when he didn't want to engage in conversation. Wendy, on the other hand, was very keen to talk.

'It all just seems a bit odd. Hearing it on the news on the radio and phoning it in because his ex-wife owned a similar top and ring. I mean, I know, that's why we put the appeals out in the first place, but still. Bit weird, isn't it? That suddenly, I mean.'

This was almost becoming a game to Wendy now. Although she respected her boss, she did take a perverse pleasure in making him feel uncomfortable.

'How long until we ask him for an alibi for last night? Sad to say it, but he's the only lead we've got at the moment. It probably won't have crossed his mind yet, but we should speak to him before he's had a chance to think about it. I'll wait for the FLO to see him first, though.'

'I can speak to him if you'd like,' she added. 'Presume you'll be sending Debbie as the FLO?' DC Debbie Weston was the trained Family Liaison Officer for the department. 'That's one job I'd never want to do. Not exactly many bright days in that job, are there?'

Culverhouse let out a sigh. 'Helen came to see me last night.'

Wendy's eyebrows shot up as the traffic lights turned green and the car stuttered forward, her foot slipping off the clutch a little too keenly. 'Helen? Your wife Helen?'

'Yeah.'

'What did she say? What did she want? Where's she been?'

'Nothing of any use, God knows, and Spain, apparently.'

'Blimey,' Wendy said, unsure of what else to say. 'I hope she had her excuses at the ready.'

'Oh yes. Plenty of excuses. As per usual,' Culverhouse replied, looking out of the passenger-side window.

'I'm not really sure what to say. How do you feel?'

'Tired.'

Wendy nodded. She could only remember one other time when she'd been in this position, Jack opening up and telling her something other than how many sugars he wanted in his coffee.

'I'll speak to Debbie when we get back,' he said, changing the subject. 'I'll let her know the situation so she knows we'll want to speak to Quinn. Get her to keep her eyes and ears open.'

Wendy desperately wanted to know more about Helen's visit but could see Jack didn't want to talk about it. Now that she thought about it, she realised he hadn't ever even told her about Helen leaving or what had happened. She'd only heard the third-hand stories that everyone else had, that Helen had upped and left one day with their young daughter. Most people knew better than to broach the subject and ask what happened. Culverhouse could be a terrifying character at the best of times, so asking him why his wife had walked out on him and taken their daughter with her didn't seem like a great idea to most people.

So why had he suddenly trusted her? Perhaps he just needed to tell someone, she presumed. A man like Jack Culverhouse didn't have many close friends, living his life wedded to the job. She presumed he had just needed to open up and she left it at that.

9

Keira Quinn's flat wasn't what Wendy would've called luxurious. Ambassador Court was a stone's throw from the town centre, which was about the only thing it had going for it.

The flat was small, cramped and dirty. It seemed as though Keira had done her best to keep it tidy as best she could, but the rising damp, peeling plaster and grubby decor seemed to indicate that the landlord had been less than attentive in his duties.

Aside from a decent-sized flat-screen television, Keira Quinn seemed to have lived a fairly simple and modest existence. Wendy knew that a flat in Ambassador Court would cost around four to five hundred pounds a month in the current market.

DS Steve Wing was looking into her financial affairs, but Andy Quinn had mentioned in the car on the way to the mortuary that his ex-wife didn't have a full-time job. If Keira had been in receipt of jobseeker's allowance — something Steve would be able to ascertain — she'd only get £73 a week, which would barely cover her rent, let alone anything else. And due to the government's stringent restrictions on out-of-work benefits she'd have to jump through all sorts of hoops and meet eligibility targets on job applications.

Wendy looked out of the living room window at the street below. The traffic was, as usual, backed up from the town centre and the noise was audible throughout the flat. So much for peace and tranquility, she thought.

Culverhouse was busy looking through the opened mail which'd been stacked neatly on the small drop-leaf dining table. There seemed to be nothing particularly interesting; a mobile phone bill for £28.30, a letter from a local jeweller's advertising a closing-down sale and a request for her to come and give blood next month. Wendy chuckled at the dark humour. Keira Quinn had given more than enough blood last night.

'Amazing, isn't it?' Culverhouse said. 'Absolutely nothing here to tell us who she was or what she was up to. No payslips, no photos, no bills lying around other than the mobile phone one.'

'Maybe not everyone's as disorganised as you,' Wendy said with a smile. 'If she lived a fairly simple life there's no reason why she should have loads of paperwork lying around the flat. Probably enough time to keep it tidy, too, if she wasn't working.'

'Just seems a bit odd to me,' Culverhouse said. He had an uncanny way of dropping a little seed of a hint into conversations, knowing full well that it would germinate in the other person's mind and end up having to be addressed anyway, whether they liked it or not.

'Maybe she kept it all digitally. It's not a massive place, so maybe she just liked to keep everything tidy and minimalistic. Many people do. Anyway, if she wasn't working, what sort of paperwork would she have? Gas, electric and water are probably all online. Mine are, as is my mobile phone bill. I think the only bill I get through the post is the council tax once a year.'

'Yeah, but no junk mail, nothing?'

'She might be on the Royal Mail list.'

'That doesn't mean a bloody thing. I'm on it and I still get half the Amazon fucking rainforest through my letterbox every week.'

Wendy chuckled inwardly, having had an unavoidable image of groups of local youths signing Culverhouse up for every imaginable piece of junk mail in existence.

The forensics team had already been to the flat to check for any signs of forced entry as well as to test for blood stains and any other signs that Keira had been killed in her flat. Everything seemed to indicate that she hadn't been.

'Always amazes me how tidy they leave a place, that lot,' Culverhouse said. 'You know, they could just say they've been to a scene and done their swabs and shit and no-one would be any the wiser. Makes you wonder.'

Wendy chose to ignore his comment, assuming it to be another attempt at being inflammatory.

They spent fifteen minutes looking around the flat but could find absolutely nothing of interest. That, in itself, was something of interest as it seemed that Keira Quinn lived a far simpler life than even the most minimalist of people. The flat was almost eerie — a complete lack of personal touches. It seemed to Wendy to be more like a show home than somewhere that people actually lived.

Uniformed officers had spoken to the occupants of the neighbouring flats to see if anyone remembered seeing her coming or going over the past couple of days but none of them were able to provide any information. A number of neighbours confirmed that Keira did live in the flat and that they tended to see her regularly, which put paid to the nagging doubt in Wendy's mind that the flat didn't even look lived in. Perhaps she was just an incredibly neat and organised person after all.

But that didn't help them in terms of uncovering clues which could lead them towards discovering who might have wanted to kill her. Other than her mutilated body, Keira Quinn seemed to have managed to stay more or less untraceable, even in death.

10

1ST SEPTEMBER

The morning sun was far brighter than either Wendy Knight's or Jack Culverhouse's moods, searing through the vertical blinds like a laser beam as Culverhouse shielded his eyes while he addressed the incident room.

'Right. Report's in from the post mortem,' he said as the other officers looked on. 'Might as well have not bothered as there's nothing new other than an estimated time of death, which they put at somewhere between midnight and one o'clock in the morning, although there were some inconsistencies. We should get more detail later today, with any luck. Luke, any luck with the CCTV?'

The eyes of the officers darted over to DS Luke Baxter, who was leaning back on his chair, twiddling a pencil around in his mouth. At the sound of his name, he dropped his chair forward and sat up.

'Nothing yet, guv. Nothing council-owned anywhere near there. Nearest ones are on the high street, in the square. Quite a few people on that, though, so we'd need to narrow it down. Frank and Debbie have been doing door-to-door and have been asking if anyone's got private CCTV installed but don't think they've had any luck so far.'

'Nope, nothing,' DS Frank Vine confirmed. 'No-one seems to have heard anything either, apart from one elderly woman who says she heard what sounded like a van pulling up outside her house around two-thirty yesterday morning.'

'Where does she live?' Culverhouse asked, signalling to DC Debbie Weston to pull the cord and close the blinds.

'About a hundred yards from where the body was found. Would be a long way to drag it, especially without leaving traces. Risky, too. Anyone could've looked out their window, come out of their house, anything. And you'd expect some sort of trace if she'd been dragged. Bits of clothing or skin on the pavement, marks on the body, something in the mud. Forensics say they couldn't find anything.'

'So how do they reckon she got there?'

'Carried, probably, but they can't be sure. They can only say she wasn't dragged. Problem is it's all paved round there, so there's no mud or grass for indentations. To put it bluntly, he could've used anything from a wheelbarrow to a forklift truck and we'd have the same amount of trace evidence — bugger all.'

'The van's got to be worth looking into, though,' Culverhouse replied. 'Check the CCTV on the high street for vans passing in the hour before and after. See if you can get any registrations. No other neighbours heard anything?'

'Nothing that they remember,' Frank replied.

'I did find something interesting, though,' DS Steve Wing cut in. 'I got onto Keira Quinn's bank yesterday after she was identified, trying to track her last movements. There were no transactions since the twenty-seventh other than the usual direct debits. Nothing manual. But I looked further back while I was there and I did spot something tasty. It seems her ex-husband, a Mr A. P. Quinn, had been paying regular payments into her account for the past few years. A hundred pounds every week, in fact. But that suddenly stopped about three weeks ago.'

'Interesting,' Culverhouse said. 'Very interesting. When we spoke to Andy Quinn he said they were divorced three years ago. And they don't have any kids. So why would he be paying her money each week?'

'Exactly what I thought,' Steve replied. 'That's what I'd be asking him if I were you.'

'Well I'm glad I'm not,' Culverhouse said. 'Either way, I think we need to have another word with Mr Quinn.'

11

Their visit to Andy Quinn's home was timed to see them arrive ten minutes after Debbie Weston, the FLO. Arriving mob-handed wouldn't have got them off to a good start and having a trusted officer in Debbie Weston about the place was intended to put Quinn at ease.

'I'm sure DC Weston has already updated you on the news from forensics and the door-to-door enquiries, Mr Quinn, but we need to double-check a few things with you and ask you some questions pertaining to operational procedure,' Wendy said diplomatically. She'd already tactically suggested that perhaps she should take the lead in speaking to Quinn, knowing Culverhouse's tendency for being tactless.

'Yes, of course. I'll do what I can to help,' Quinn said, forcing a smile.

'I'm sure you understand that we've had to look into Keira's personal life quite closely in order to establish the circumstances leading to her death. As part of that, we had to go through her bank statements to see who she was financially linked to. We saw a number of payments, every week in fact, from your account to hers over a number of years. What were these for?'

Quinn turned his head towards the window and Wendy saw his jaw clenching.

'I'd been paying her some money to keep her going. I don't exactly have much, but it was certainly more than she had. I felt some sort of obligation towards her and didn't want to see her out on the streets. You didn't know her like I did. She was a heavy drinker and hadn't worked a day in her life. That's what we argued about, a lot of the time. Despite all that I still cared for her, of course I did. So I used to give her some money out of my pay packet to make sure she wasn't lying in a gutter somewhere.'

'Why did you stop the payments?' Wendy asked, hoping to catch Quinn in a stream of opening up.

He made a small snorting noise. 'Because I found out she'd been earning an income after all. A friend told me that Keira had been working as a hooker for a few months. When I asked her, she admitted it. As I saw it, not only did she have an income but she'd broken my trust. That's when I put a stop to the payments.'

'So when you told us yesterday that she didn't work, you were lying,' Culverhouse said.

'It's not work, is it? Not full-time, anyway. And certainly not what you could call a career option. I didn't see much point in mentioning it. She might as well have some dignity left.'

'That's not really for you to judge,' Culverhouse replied. 'How did she take you stopping the payments? I mean, I can imagine she'd've been pretty pissed off.'

'She wasn't exactly happy, no,' Quinn replied, brushing an invisible speck of dust from the arm of his chair. 'She said it was her life and she'd do as she pleased. I agreed and said I'd do what I wanted with mine too. We agreed to disagree.'

'Very diplomatically put,' Culverhouse said.

Wendy cut in before he could say any more. 'Now we've got to ask, as I'm sure you imagine — do you know of anyone who would've wanted Keira dead?'

Quinn looked at the floor and seemed to be genuinely trying to rack his brains. 'No, nobody. No-one that I can think of. But then again we didn't exactly speak to each other much since we were divorced, so I wouldn't know anyone she'd met since.'

'You didn't speak, but you paid a hundred quid a week into her bank account,' Culverhouse said, raising an eyebrow.

'I've already explained that,' Quinn replied, staring Culverhouse down. 'Is it a crime to want your ex-wife not to live on the streets?'

'I'm not sure I'd be quite as caring,' Culverhouse replied.

'Well that goes to show that we're very different people, doesn't it?'

'It certainly does. Where were you on the night of the thirtieth and morning of the thirty-first of August, Andy?' Culverhouse liked to try and catch people off-guard in the vain hope that a suspect might slip up or at least give in to a slight, subconscious facial twitch — a 'tell' which would belie their words.

'I was at home. And before you ask, no, I don't have an alibi. I was at home on my own, watching TV all evening and then I went to bed.'

'Anything good on?' Culverhouse asked.

'Not especially, no. Usual rubbish.'

'Which programmes did you watch?' Wendy asked, a little more directly than Culverhouse had.

'Uh, I think there was something about Indian cookery.

Yeah, I remember that one because it made me hungry and I ended up making some cheese on toast. The slice of bread is still missing from the pack if you want to check that.'

Culverhouse gave him an icy stare. 'And then what? Off to bed with a mug of Horlicks and a copy of the Reader's Digest?'

'If you like. I woke up in the morning, put the radio on while I was making my breakfast and that's when I heard about the body.'

'Making your breakfast at nine in the morning?' Culverhouse asked. 'Wouldn't you have been at work by then?'

'I had a day off,' Quinn replied, looking at Culverhouse with a neutral look in his eyes.

'To do what?'

'To relax. We all need to relax now and again, don't we? Turned out not to be very relaxing at all.'

Wendy could sense the tension growing between Quinn and Culverhouse and decided to try and defuse it.

'If you could possibly have a think for us and let us know if you think of anyone who might be able to provide an alibi, please let us know. Perhaps a neighbour who saw you outside, a friend who called — anything like that.'

'I will,' Quinn said, smiling at Wendy. 'Thank you.'

'Something's not quite right there,' Culverhouse said when they'd left and were getting back into their car. 'The thing with the payments is just bloody weird. And no alibi? And having a day off work? Handy, that.'

'I'm not quite sure how,' Wendy replied. 'Surely if he'd killed her he'd want to make everything look as normal as possible to divert suspicion away from him.'

'Dunno about that. We've both known our fair share of killers who delight in the chase, trying to get us to suspect them while just keeping any decent evidence out of reach.'

'You reckon?' Wendy asked, pulling away from the kerb.

'Come on, Knight. You saw the way he looked at me. Almost goading me, boasting with his eyes.'

'That probably had more to do with the fact that you were being less than sensitive, as usual. I'm surprised you didn't ask him where the murder weapon was.'

'Of course, I forgot we were meant to be treating murder suspects with respect. Like the respect he showed Keira Quinn when he sliced her fucking neck open.'

'You don't know that he did, guv. Doesn't quite sound right to me that he'd risk all that for no reason. They were divorced, he wasn't paying her money each week any more. What reason could he have for killing her?'

Culverhouse looked out of the side window of the car and exhaled, his breath steaming up on the glass. 'That's what I intend to find out.'

Jack Culverhouse flicked through the reports that'd been left on his desk by Frank Vine. The door-to-door enquiries had thrown up nothing and speaking to Keira Quinn's few friends and family had given them half as much.

On closer inspection it seemed that Keira hadn't been working as a street prostitute, but rather as a private escort. There was no trace of any records of clients at her flat, so any link between her professional life and her death would be speculative at best.

It was a sad fact of life that prostitutes were far more likely to be murdered than most other people. With so many street prostitutes in Britain coming from migrant communities, it was likely that hundreds, if not thousands more died each year than were officially recorded.

Culverhouse took another sip of his steaming coffee. All of the details about Keira's life seemed to show that no-one would have a reason for wanting her dead, yet the manner of her murder showed evidence of being a very deliberate act. Unless somebody was out to deliberately target prostitutes and escorts, something didn't quite add up.

In his mind, the only real explanation was that Andy Quinn had to be involved somewhere along the line. On the face of things he may have had no reason to want his ex-wife dead, but the fact was they only had his word for it. Keira Quinn seemingly kept herself to herself and not many people knew much about her. It wouldn't be beyond the realms of possibility for Andy Quinn to be hiding something from them.

As Culverhouse tried to think through some possibilities, the phone on his desk began to ring. A withheld number. He picked it up.

'Culverhouse?'

The voice on the other end of the phone wasn't one he recognised.

'DCI Culverhouse? My name's Suzanne Corrigan, I'm a reporter on the Mildenheath Gazette. I was just wondering if I might be able to ask you a couple of questions. It's about the Keira Quinn murder. We're running a story on it this week and I—'

'I don't recognise your name,' Culverhouse interrupted. He made it his business to know the names of the reporters on the local newspapers. If he was perfectly honest, he found it hard to avoid them.

'You probably won't. I'm new,' Suzanne said. 'Now, I just wanted to clarify whether—'

'The only information I release will be at press conferences or managed press releases, Ms Corrigan,' Culverhouse replied. 'If there's anything we want to release to the public I'll be sure to let you know.'

Culverhouse was about to put the phone down when he heard something that caught his interest.

'Is it true that Keira Quinn was working as an escort?'

He raised the phone back to his ear. 'Who told you that?'

'Is it true?' Suzanne Corrigan repeated.

Culverhouse paused while he considered his response. 'If we have any further information we'll organise a press conference or issue a press release.'

He put the phone down before Suzanne Corrigan could say any more. His relationship with the press and media outlets had always been conflicted. There were times when he was annoyed at their constant intrusion into investigations, but then there were also times when they truly came in useful, such as bringing Andy Quinn to their attention so quickly. Right now, though, he was more upset that a local journalist could be about to publish information which would harm their investigation.

He put down his mug of coffee and stepped out of his office to address the incident room.

'Did anyone by any chance happen to accidentally tell a fucking reporter that Keira Quinn was a hooker?'

His question was met with silence, save for a couple of small chuckles from officers who found Culverhouse's flair for language amusing.

'Right,' he said after a few seconds. 'I'll take that as a no. Which means one of you fuckers is lying to me, because I fail to see how a desk monkey at the Gazette could've found that out so quickly seeing as it took them six years to work out their editor was a paedo.' A previous editor of the Mildenheath Gazette, Denis Rowe, had been uncovered as a predatory paedophile a few years earlier — a scandal which almost sunk the newspaper. 'Knight, if you could peel your face away from that computer screen and come and see me in my office, I've got a few things I need to update you on.'

'Uh yeah, no problem, guv,' Wendy replied, looking up from her computer. 'But I just need to finish this. Can I have five minutes?'

Culverhouse grunted. 'You can have ten. I'm going for a shit.'

13

4TH SEPTEMBER

Culverhouse had been thinking about calling Helen for a number of days. Ever since she'd left his house a few nights back, in fact. It seemed incongruous to him that her having disappeared from his life for so long should just be explained away with a couple of hours of vague excuses and bickering. He was used to getting explanations out of people and gaining a full oversight of situations, and his marriage was going to be no different.

He didn't want to be the one to go running to her — that would look too desperate — but at the same time he was well aware that if he didn't call her then she wouldn't be in any great rush to be the one to initiate contact. Her actions over the past few years had proved that.

Cautiously, he pulled his mobile phone out of his pocket, unlocked it and tapped in the number Helen had written down and handed to him. There was a few seconds of silence before the phone finally started ringing. Helen picked up after only two rings.

'It's me,' Culverhouse said, not sure what else to say. He'd been thinking about this for days but still hadn't come any closer to knowing which words to use.

'Hi,' Helen replied, characteristically vague and non-committal.

'I just wanted to try and smooth things over a bit. After the other night.'

'Jack Culverhouse the peacemaker. Well I never.'

Helen's barbed reply didn't surprise him, but it still hurt.

'Like you said, people change. And in case you hadn't noticed, we've got a child together. I think it's probably best we at least try to be civil, don't you?' Culverhouse could feel the anger rising inside him as he tried to suppress it. Getting worked up wouldn't do him any favours. It rarely did, but this time he knew he had too much to lose. All Helen would have to do is ditch the mobile phone and she'd be uncontactable again — possibly forever.

Although he was desperate to see his daughter and was never one to worry about breaking the rules, Culverhouse had always stopped short of using police resources to find his wife. Technically speaking, what Helen had done was parental child abduction, but it was far more complicated than that. At the time, he didn't even know for sure that she'd left the country.

Jack knew he was not without his foibles, to say the least. Deep down, he'd always known that Emily was probably far better off in another country with Helen than she was forced to live with both parents, her father barely ever at home and coming under growing stress at work.

As much as he wanted Emily back and could've pulled rank to have her found, something deep and primal was telling him that it wouldn't have been the best thing for his daughter. Jack Culverhouse wasn't usually the first person to be self-deprecating, but he knew he wasn't going to be winning any Father of the Year awards.

Over the years, this had manifested itself into immense guilt. The more time that passed without him having gone out and searched for Emily, or at least having made a couple of phone calls to verify that she was safe, the more he berated himself over it and the less legitimate a claim he felt he had. The passing of time was not something he could do anything about.

'I'm willing to be civil, Jack, but I'm not willing to be emotionally abused,' Helen's voice said as Culverhouse held the phone to his ear. 'I deserve better than that. Emily deserves better than that.'

He couldn't disagree with that. 'I know. Look, this hasn't exactly been an easy situation for any of us, has it? You turning up out of the blue took me by surprise. Things haven't been easy lately, but I honestly was pleased to see you.' Not for the first time, he wished he'd thought before he spoke.

'Really?' came the only word from Helen.

'Yeah. I mean, I didn't know what had happened to you. We're still married, Helen. That means something.'

'Why did you never try to find me, Jack?' Helen said after a few moments' silence.

He tried not to get too defensive. 'The burden wasn't really on me. It wasn't a game of hide and seek. I see this sort of thing happening all the time in my job and the battles can go on for years. The only people who lose out are the kids. I didn't want that for Emily. I guess I thought that things would work themselves out eventually. And they have. Sort of.'

'You're such a man. You know, you could've had Interpol find us and arrest us if you'd really wanted to.'

'I know that,' he replied. 'And like I said, I can't imagine that would've been the best thing for Emily. I was left to choose between two shitty choices, neither of which I wanted. I had to choose what was best for everyone else rather than thinking selfishly and doing what was best for me.'

'Well there's a first for everything,' Helen replied.

Culverhouse closed his eyes. 'That's unfair, Helen.'

'You're right. I'm sorry,' came the reply. 'Listen, we should meet up and talk. Properly. Discuss it like adults.'

Although he'd have to tread on eggshells, Culverhouse finally felt as though he might be getting somewhere. He'd have to swallow his pride — he knew that. If it meant that he'd get to see Emily, it would be worth every second.

14

Culverhouse had agreed to meet Helen at a coffee shop in the outdoor shopping precinct in the middle of Mildenheath. The shop was from a large national chain — the sort Culverhouse despised, seeing as all he wanted was a straight black coffee; not a cappuccino, cafe latte or macchiato — whatever the hell they were.

Although the weather had turned chillier than it had been recently, hordes of people were still sitting at the outside tables, clutching at their warm mugs of coffee, such was the novelty of a coffee terrace in Mildenheath.

Fortunately for him, Helen wasn't one of those. She'd positioned herself in the corner of the coffee shop, near the disabled toilet and far enough away from the counter to avoid the temptation of the cakes and biscuits on offer.

He made his way over to the counter and ordered a 'normal coffee' before sitting down at the table with Helen.

'I thought you were ill,' Helen said, before having even said hello.

'Sorry?'

'When you rang to apologise. I presumed you must've been ill or something. I don't think in all our years of marriage I've ever heard you apologise.'

'I didn't apologise,' Culverhouse replied, shifting in his seat. 'I wanted to smooth things over.'

'Well I guess that's a start.'

He could feel the blood pressure rising in his temples but decided not to give in to it and instead tried to remain as calm as he could.

'Do you want to talk about it?' he asked, hoping he sounded caring and sympathetic. 'About your problems, I mean.'

Helen said nothing for a few moments and instead sat stirring a wooden stick around in her cappuccino. 'I'm not sure what you want me to say.'

'Is there anything I can do to help?' he asked.

She shook her head and Culverhouse could've sworn he heard a slight chuckle. 'I doubt it very much. There's the medication, but that only takes the edge off things. It's not a long-term solution.'

'What is?'

'I dunno. Behavioural therapies. CBT. Counselling.'

'Counselling?' Culverhouse asked. 'For what?'

'Oh, I don't mean counselling like for trauma or anything, but just general talking about stuff. Not keeping it all bottled up. Learning to deal with thought processes, that kind of thing.'

Culverhouse thought it all sounded like a load of wishy-washy mumbo jumbo but he didn't want to say anything.

'And will that help?' he asked. 'Long term, I mean.'

'Who knows? Your guess is as good as anybody's. Got to be better than doing nothing, though.'

He desperately wanted to know more but wasn't sure what

questions to ask. 'What about from day to day? What effect does it have on things?'

Helen raised one corner of her mouth. 'Hopefully very little. Not as much as it did at one point, anyway. If there's a stressful situation it'll be worse but it's pretty manageable at the moment.'

'So you don't need help?'

'Of course I need help. I'll always need help. It's not easy, but it's not as bad as it was.' Helen was silent for a few moments before speaking again. 'I mean, I'm not saying things could necessarily go back to normal, but I'm doing my best, Jack.'

Culverhouse looked up from his coffee in surprise. 'I wasn't... I wasn't trying to suggest anything. I didn't mean that.'

'No, I know you didn't,' Helen replied. Culverhouse tried to detect the subtext but couldn't.

'I just want to get things sorted,' he replied. 'For Emily's sake.'

Helen nodded.

Culverhouse continued. 'I just want to see her, Hel. I've missed nearly three quarters of her life. That's... That's hard.'

'Well it wasn't exactly a barrel of laughs for us either,' Helen replied, acid-tongued.

'I know,' he replied, not knowing at all. 'I can only imagine. But things are moving on, aren't they? I mean, you're back here and we're talking and being adults, so why can't I see her?'

'Because I'm not ready for you to.'

He could feel his blood pressure rising again. He tried not to react, to show that he could rise above his primal reactions, but he was struggling more and more.

'Is she ready?' he asked, trying as hard as he could not to allow any of the anger and frustration come out in his voice.

'I don't know.'

'Well I am. I'm more than ready. I'll do whatever it takes.'

'I already said I don't know, Jack,' Helen replied, her voice raised. 'I need time, alright? Now are we going to talk or are you just going to keep going over the same old ground?'

Culverhouse picked up the small biscotti that had been given to him on the saucer with his coffee. He bit down hard, unsure as to whether the resultant crack was from the rock-hard biscuit or one of his teeth. It was the closest he could come to whacking a punchbag.

He wasn't stupid — he knew Helen didn't want him to keep going on about Emily, but at the same time he'd had enough of being walked all over by her. She'd been firmly in control of his life for the past eight and a half years without even being there, and he'd long since stopped caring for her feelings. He was only placating her to get access to Emily.

'I just want to see her, that's all.'

Helen shot up onto her feet, the table clattering as she did so. 'You don't fucking get it, do you? You can't help yourself.'

Culverhouse could feel the eyes of the other coffee shop customers boring into him. 'Helen, I—'

'No, Jack. You won't change. You're not capable of changing. If you want to see Emily, you can damn well whistle.'

He didn't bother to look up and watch her walk out of the shop. He just sat and stared into the remains of his coffee, sensing the eyes of the other customers leaving him and the hubbub of conversation returning to normal.

15

Culverhouse had always hoped that Helen would return one day, but he'd always imagined Emily would have been with her. He'd tried to imagine how she might look, but his vision had always reverted to the bubbly, giggling three-year-old she was when he last saw her.

For eight and a half years he'd always had the option to pull rank and use his position to have Helen and Emily traced down, but he'd resisted. He'd always hoped there'd be a better way; a more honest way. Now, though, he realised his options were far more limited and had decided to do just that.

He'd worked with Inspector Antonio García on a cross-border case a few years back and had struck up an immediate rapport with him. García operated in a similar way to Culverhouse, always ensuring that justice was achieved — even if a few rules had to be broken along the way.

García was based in Alicante, on the eastern coast of Spain. It wasn't where Helen had said she had been living, but Alicante was certainly closer than Mildenheath and García was someone Culverhouse knew he could trust.

He picked up his personal mobile and dialled García's number. The Inspector's superb grasp of English and love of British idioms was immediately familiar to Culverhouse.

'Jack, good to hear from you! How's it going?' came the cheery voice on the other end of the phone.

'Not bad, but not great. Hence why I'm calling you,' Culverhouse said.

'Ah-ha, I see. You want me to do you another favour, yes?' García replied.

'Yeah, I do. Only this time it's got to stay off the record.'

García didn't reply for a few moments. 'What's it all about, Jack?' he finally replied.

'I'm sending a photo to your personal email address. It's of a woman who's supposedly living in southern Spain. I need to find out where. She's with a young girl who's almost eleven. Possibly also with a guy called David, who I don't have a description of.'

'What does the girl look like?' García asked.

'I don't know,' Culverhouse replied, feeling the impact of his own words. 'I mean, I know what she used to look like. Eight and a half years ago.'

'Kids grow up quick,' García said. 'I doubt she'll look like that any more. What's the woman's name?'

Culverhouse sighed. 'Helen. Helen Culverhouse.'

García made a noise which told him that he'd cottoned on. Culverhouse had told him a few years back over a drunken night in Alicante that he had a wife and daughter who'd left him, but hadn't gone into any details. Not that he could remember, anyway.

'Are you sure this is wise, Jack?'

'Yeah. Don't worry, I'm not doing anything stupid.'

'How do I know that's true?' García asked.

'Because I just told you. I wouldn't do anything to risk any harm coming to Emily.'

'That's the daughter?'

'Yes. That's my daughter.'

'Right,' García said. 'And whereabouts in Spain are they meant to be?'

'Southern,' Culverhouse replied. 'I don't know where exactly.'

García let out his distinctive chuckle. 'Jack, do you know how big Spain is? The south coast is over five hundred kilometres long. You'll need to narrow it down a bit, my friend. She could be in Sevilla, Almería, Málaga, anywhere. She could even be in Gibraltar.'

'No, not Gibraltar,' Culverhouse said. 'She said she was in Spain.'

'Hey hey, don't go starting that shit,' García replied. Culverhouse had to laugh at his distinctly English turn of phrase.

'What I mean is I got the impression she was on the mainland.'

'You spoke to her?'

'Yeah,' Culverhouse replied, realising he was probably going to have to explain the whole situation if García was going to be able to help him effectively. 'She came back. To England. She's here now.'

'So what's the problem? You've found her.'

'I don't want her. I want Emily. My daughter.'

'And she won't let you see her?'

'No. I think that ship's sailed.'

'So why did she come back?' García asked.

'I don't know. I really don't fucking know. To rub my nose in it, probably. Just in case I'd started to get over it or something. I don't know what she's playing at. And right now I don't care. I always thought Emily was safer with Helen, somehow better off. But she's not. I've got to be honest, Antonio. I think she's in danger.'

'Danger? How so?'

Culverhouse sighed loudly. 'Helen's mentally unstable. She's on medication and has violent mood swings.' He realised he was now exaggerating wildly, but sometimes strings had to be pulled. 'If I'm completely honest, I don't even know that Emily's safe as it is. Helen said she was with some guy called David — I don't know if he's English or Spanish — and I certainly don't have a bloody clue who he is. For all I know he could be dangerous too.'

'Alright Jack, alright,' García said, trying to placate him. 'Listen, I'll see what I can do, okay? I'll speak to a few people. There are a few ex-pat communities on the south coast. I'll try those first and see if I can find anything, but looking for a British family on the south coast of Spain is like trying to find a grain of sand on a beach. We have to hope she's using her real name over here, otherwise it's going to be difficult to say the least.'

'You'll circulate her photo, too?' Culverhouse asked.

'I can do, but that all depends on how off-the-record this is meant to be. If you want it kept under the radar I can't go sending photos around all the police departments.'

Culverhouse thought for a few moments. 'I understand. Thanks, Antonio. Just let me know if you find anything. I'll see what I can do at this end too, but at the moment you're my best hope.'

'Hey, I'll remember that. Once this is sorted out, you get yourself over here and you can buy me a few beers, *entiendes?*'

Culverhouse smiled for the first time in a long time.

16

The man opened the wooden gate and ushered the woman through. She teetered unsteadily as her heels tapped softly along the paving stones before opting for the near silence of soft grass.

'I've never done it in someone's garden before,' she giggled as she turned and watched him close the gate behind him. 'Kind of exciting, don't you think?'

'Certainly is,' the man replied, the grin covering every inch of his face. 'More than you'll ever know.'

She hadn't been the most difficult conquest of his life. The way she'd stood at the bar had said a thousand words alone, and he'd already heard a good few stories about this woman to know that he was pretty much assured of a good time. Unfortunately for her, his idea of a good time was far removed from most other people's.

He'd chosen his time and place carefully. This was all a game of odds. His chances of success could rest on the opening of a door or the recognition of a face, which was why he'd taken great time and care over timings, places and, most importantly, ensuring he remained the master of disguise.

It had worked out beautifully. He hadn't let her get too close just yet; that could've alerted her to his wig or prosthetics. It also had the added bonus of making her wild with intrigue. Keeping his distance had worked wonders in terms of persuading her to come with him in the first place.

Under cover of darkness, though, he was safe. His disguise wouldn't be blown, and if it was he could end this in seconds. It wouldn't be the same careful and meticulously planned method that he was intending, but it would be better than the alternative.

He could smell the alcohol seeping out of her pores like black smog from a power station. She started to move closer to him, the pungent fug making his eyes water. He closed his eyes and remembered that this was a means to an end. There was no shame in what no-one knew. Besides that, there was no other way.

She moaned and groaned as she rubbed herself up against him. It was now or never. He could swear he heard another gasp of perverted pleasure as he clamped his hand over her mouth, the other holding the back of her head still so as not to allow her to move away. He looked deep into her eyes as he steadily moved her backwards towards the fence.

As he heard the thud of her back hitting the wooden panel, he allowed her a half-step forward before taking the hand from the back of her head and dropping it inside his coat pocket. The coat was brand new, as were all his clothes. A shame, but also a necessity.

'Now, are you going to be quiet for me?' he said, trying to

spot the point at which her sexual excitement turned to desperate fear.

She nodded. He could tell she was still deluded; still excited. He felt the cold, hard steel in his coat pocket before removing it, lifting it up to her throat and drawing it across, deep and firm. The warm liquid ran over his hand, making him shiver in the night. She'd had her moment. Now it was time for his pleasure.

She tried to gasp despairingly, the hole in her trachea wheezing and gurgling as he continued to clamp his hand over her mouth. By now her lungs would be pooling with blood. It was only a matter of time before he could let go, her eyes glazing over like marbles as the last vestiges of life slipped away.

Finally, he recognised those familiar signs and felt her body weaken as her legs started to give way. Using the last of her natural strength and support, he moved her back towards the fence again and let go, her body sliding down the wooden panel just as he'd intended.

He stood back and waited for her to die before tugging at her feet, making her lie almost horizontally. He pulled her feet back towards her pelvis, splaying her legs like a woman in the midst of giving birth. He took the handkerchief from his trouser pocket, shoved it in her mouth, then took it out and tied it around her neck. A slight deviation from the perfect version, but he couldn't afford to be too fussy.

Surveying his handiwork, he again drew the sharp tool from his coat pocket and this time went to work on her abdomen, having memorised each line and incision he needed to make. The firm resistance of the muscle wall was strangely satisfying, as was feeling it give way when the sharp blade finally managed to pierce through the barrier.

A few moments later, he was happy. The distant sound of a car rumbled in the distance, but other than that all was quiet.

17

8TH SEPTEMBER

Meadow Hill Lane wasn't a road the police were called to often. The tree-lined road was home to large detached houses which generally managed to keep free of the local grip of crime, other than the odd burglary or domestic incident.

Knight and Culverhouse only ever tended to come to the road when visiting Gary McCann, a local businessman who was usually less than honest in his business dealings. Rumour had it that McCann had seen his ex-wife disposed of a few years back, but this had never been proven. Much to Culverhouse's chagrin, he'd never been able to nail anything on McCann.

For the first time in a long time, though, they were on Meadow Hill Lane for a reason other than Gary McCann. They were at number twenty-nine, one of the few houses not to be given a pretentious name such as 'The Sycamores' or 'Dovedale'.

Number twenty-nine was on the corner at the roundabout where Meadow Hill Lane was bisected by another road, effectively giving the owners an impressive corner plot. The low crime level in the area meant that they tended to leave the side gate into their garden unlocked — something which they were now regretting very much.

Culverhouse glanced his eye over the dead body. It appeared to be a woman in her forties, her legs drawn up, knees splayed and her left arm placed across her chest. It struck Culverhouse as being almost sexual, although Janet Grey had assured Culverhouse that it seemed there was no immediate sign of sexual interference. Her abdomen had been slashed open, but it seemed that the cause of death was the deep laceration to her throat.

Again, a murder seemed to have been carried out within spitting distance of Mildenheath Police Station, which was barely a quarter of a mile further down the road.

'Looks as if she was attacked while standing,' Dr Grey said. 'See the fence there? The blood starts higher up and is smeared down. I'd say she fell or was pushed against the fence and slid down it, smearing the blood.' The pathologist demonstrated the likely direction of the fall with her hand.

'And it was the injury to her neck that killed her?'

'I'd say so. Can't be certain just yet, but judging by where most of the blood has come from I'd say so.'

'Any idea who she is?' Wendy asked, having been briefed by one of the first response officers while Culverhouse was talking to Dr Grey.

'Lindsay Stott, according to her driving licence,' the pathologist replied. 'She lives on James Street.'

Wendy shot a look at Culverhouse. James Street was parallel to Albert Road, where the body of Keira Quinn had been found. Culverhouse looked closely at the driving licence that Dr Grey had just handed him.

'The constable didn't say anything about this,' Wendy said,

gesturing at the young officer who she'd been speaking to moments earlier.

'That's because he didn't ask,' Dr Grey replied. Technically speaking, the constable's main priority would've been to protect and secure the scene while CID and forensics arrived.

Wendy decided to leave Culverhouse to deal with the forensics side of things while she went to speak to the home-owner, a couple in their mid-sixties who were sat in their conservatory, the husband comforting his wife with a mug of sweet tea. The constable had told Wendy that the wife had discovered the body when she went out to empty the kitchen bin that morning and had been inconsolable ever since.

She'd already been told the couple's names — Dennis and Cheryl Vincent — so she introduced herself and sat at the wicker dining table in their conservatory.

'I know this must be very distressing for you, Mrs Vincent, but I'm afraid I do need to ask you a few questions.'

'I told Dennis we should lock the side gate,' the woman said. 'Nowhere's ever completely safe, I told him. I told him.' Cheryl Vincent broke down in another fit of sobbing.

Wendy placed her hand on the woman's forearm. 'If it helps, it wouldn't have made any difference to what happened. It looks like whoever did this was hell-bent on doing so. Even if you had locked your gate, it would have happened elsewhere. There's nothing you could have done.'

The woman nodded slowly and gently.

'It seems the woman's name is Lindsay Stott,' Wendy said, looking at both Mr and Mrs Vincent for any sign of recognition. 'Did you know her at all?'

They both shook their heads, but only Dennis Vincent spoke. 'No, not that I know of. Should we have?'

'I wouldn't have thought so,' Wendy said, 'but we need to check anyway. It's likely that it was just bad luck that it was your side gate that was open, but I'm sure you'll understand that we need to check every line of enquiry.'

'Yes. Yes, of course.'

Wendy continued. 'I'm afraid I need to ask you to go through what happened this morning, Mrs Vincent. I know it'll be difficult for you but I need you to tell me everything in detail.'

Cheryl Vincent swallowed hard before speaking. 'I came down into the kitchen and put the kettle on, as I do every morning. I knew the bin needed emptying so I took the bag out and went into the garden to put it in the wheelie bin, which is next to the gate. I don't think I really noticed at first, but while I was putting the bag in the bin I sort of became aware of this... shape... by the fence at the end of the garden. That's when I looked more closely and I went over and saw the blood. And her face. The look on her face.' Cheryl Vincent's shoulders started to bob up and down as she sobbed in her husband's arms.

Back in the garden, Culverhouse was being briefed on what else Janet Grey had ascertained about Lindsay Stott's death.

'I'd say she definitely died at the scene,' the pathologist said. 'Again, it looks as though our killer's got some anatomical knowledge. The cuts to her abdomen aren't just random. They're careful and considered. Almost as if he'd planned in advance what he was going to do. There's no anger or frenzy that I can see.'

Culverhouse nodded slowly. A frenzied attack would be

straightforward enough. Sudden violent crimes always left clues. Carefully planned and considered murders didn't.

'Interesting thing is the handkerchief around her neck. Apart from the fact that it's huge, it seems like it was tied there afterwards. There aren't any slash marks to the material. We'll need to do some tests on it, but it's possible it might have been used as a gag and then pulled down over her neck after she died.'

'Right. We'll start looking into her background,' Culverhouse said. 'If it's carefully planned it's likely to have been someone close to her.'

'Perhaps,' Dr Grey said, 'although I'd be skeptical. Look at this.' The pathologist lifted up Lindsay Stott's hand. 'Looks as though she had some rings on her fingers. You can see here the marks where they were, and it looks like they were tugged off pretty violently. You can see the lacerations and bruising to the fingers.'

'You're thinking a robbery?' Culverhouse asked.

'It's your job to join the dots,' the pathologist replied. 'I just show you where the dots are.'

18

By the time Culverhouse had managed to assemble everyone in the incident room for the briefing on Lindsay Stott's death, they'd already managed to fast-track DNA testing on the hand-kerchief which had been found wrapped around her neck. The results showed that — unsurprisingly — the blood on the hand-kerchief matched that of Lindsay Stott, but also that large amounts of saliva on it also belonged to her, indicating that the handkerchief had perhaps been used as a gag or at least inserted into her mouth at some point.

Knowing the identity of Lindsay Stott from the outset had been a bonus. It had allowed them to radio in to the station to have her details run through the Police National Computer. This would show them any details the police had on file for her.

Frank Vine had run the PNC check and was looking pretty proud of what he'd found.

'No convictions, but a fair few incidents. Four calls to a previous address related to domestic incidents. All involving a Paul Stott, her husband. The last time was just over three years ago, by which time they'd apparently separated and were going through a divorce. The husband had apparently come to pick something up from the house and things had turned violent.'

'Did they get divorced in the end?' Culverhouse asked.

'No idea. Nothing on our records. Would have to check Births, Deaths and Marriages.'

'Right. Either way, he's got to be our first suspect.'

'I wouldn't say so, guv,' Frank replied, chuckling to himself. 'He died a year and a half ago. I thought the same thing as you, so I looked him up. Died in a skiing accident in Saalbach-Hinterglemm in Austria while he was on holiday with his new family.'

'Blimey. There's a family that attracts good luck,' Culverhouse replied.

'I don't think Paul Stott's new family would have been all that close to Lindsay, guv. Not looking at our records. Apparently she was a heavy drinker. They both were, but it seemed to cause more problems for her. Indications of violence on both sides. He believed she'd been sleeping around and that seemed to cause most of the fights. Looks like one of those couplings that should never have been allowed to happen.'

Culverhouse nodded. He knew exactly the sort of one he meant. 'So who's left family-wise?'

'That's what I'm trying to find out. Looks like she lived alone, though. According to the electoral register, anyway.'

'Right. Keep digging,' Culverhouse said. 'Luke, Debbie, can you start door-to-door enquiries with the neighbours? Find out if anyone was seen coming or going from her house over the past couple of days. See what you can find out about her work. Steve, I'll get clearance for a search on her house. See what's there in terms of payslips or any indication of regular connections. We need to build up a picture of who Lindsay Stott was and what sort of life she lived.'

'Will you need me in contact with the Vincents, too?' Debbie asked, knowing the poor unsuspecting couple would need a family liaison officer to help them come to terms with finding a mutilated dead body in their pristine back garden.

'Yes,' Culverhouse replied, bluntly. 'It's only round the corner from James Street. And from here.'

Before anyone could say anything else, Luke Baxter jumped in. 'Are we looking at any connection between Lindsay Stott and Keira Quinn, guv?'

Culverhouse sighed. 'In terms of whether they knew each other? Worth looking into, but where do you begin? But I presume that wasn't what you meant, was it?'

Luke Baxter simply returned a cheeky smile. Wendy knew that any other superior officer would've wiped the smile off his face, but Culverhouse's infuriating soft spot for Baxter meant otherwise.

Culverhouse continued. 'There's nothing at all, concrete or otherwise, to link the two. Absolutely nothing. I don't even want the possibility mentioned outside of this room and any press enquiries or anyone asking about links, just play dumb. Shouldn't be too tricky for some of you. But within these four walls? Two single women being killed within ten days of each other and dumped in residential areas? Well, it doesn't take fucking Einstein to find that a bit weird, does it?'

19

Wendy could always more or less tell the outcome of a morning briefing before a word had even been spoken. As she walked into the incident room that morning, she could sense an atmosphere of solemn frustration.

The surviving family of Lindsay Stott had been looked into, but other than an aunt in Somerset and a few cousins dotted around the country, Lindsay had no close family. She'd been born in London, her parents both being in their fifties when she was born and both now long dead of natural causes.

The door-to-door enquiries and chats with her neighbours had proved pretty fruitless, too. None of them seemed to have known Lindsay personally other than saying hello over the front wall occasionally, although a couple mentioned that she had a pretty solid routine of leaving her house around six-thirty each evening and coming back between eleven and midnight. It was assumed she had a local pub that she frequented, and Steve Wing had graciously volunteered to visit all of Mildenheath's pubs in person to see if anyone recognised her.

The local newspapers had, predictably, already been tipped

off and would no doubt be running their own stories on the discovery of Lindsay Stott's body, but the debate now was on whether or not Mildenheath Police should hold a formal press conference.

'It'd help us find people who might have known her,' Wendy explained. 'You don't live in a town like Mildenheath for long without getting to know and recognise people. The six degrees of separation don't come into play here. It's more like two degrees in Mildenheath.'

'Only problem with that is that we don't tend to hold a formal press conference every time someone dies. It'll raise eyebrows,' Culverhouse replied.

'We do when we can't find out enough about the person ourselves. People will just assume we're looking for more information.'

'What, barely a week after another body was found? We've got nothing on that and we've got nothing on this. People'll automatically assume we're linking the two.'

'But we are, aren't we?'

'That's not the point, Knight. If there's even so much as a sniff of a rumour that we're looking for a serial killer, there'll be pandemonium. I'm not risking it.'

'You'd need three for it to be a serial killer, guv,' Luke Baxter piped up from the back of the room. 'This'd just be a double murder.'

Culverhouse stared at Baxter for a few moments. 'Fuck off, Luke.'

Wendy couldn't help but let out a snort and a laugh. Culverhouse pretended he hadn't heard and carried on speaking. 'The last thing we want to be doing is panicking people. We have enough trouble sorting the wheat from the chaff as it is. I'll give it another twenty-four hours. See what Steve finds from the local pubs and get all of the records checked and double checked. If we're really stuck, then perhaps I'll consider it.'

The sensationalist local media had a nasty habit of blowing stories out of proportion in their clamour to flog exclusives up to the national papers. Culverhouse knew from experience that they could often do far more harm than good by creating their own theories and trying to find a scapegoat, whether that be their own theories as to a suspect or simply blaming the police for incompetence.

Wendy was well aware that handling the media was one of the biggest challenges facing modern policing, particularly now that the line between the media and the general public had blurred. With the advent of smartphones and everyone having a camera and potentially a direct link to worldwide social media in their pockets, a photo of a crime scene and an accompanying theory could be sent all over the world within seconds. The protection and control of sensitive information in the digital age was now a major priority.

Only a few months earlier, Mildenheath Police had been embroiled in a scandal in which a raid on a suspected paedophile's home had been filmed by a passer-by on a smartphone, only with the added complication that the custody van had been parked a good hundred yards down the road, meaning that the handcuffed suspect had been paraded down the street in full view. By the time the case was later dropped due to insufficient evidence, the man had already seen his face plastered all over social media and had found his property vandalised and his life ruined. Six weeks later he took his own life and the police had come under intense scrutiny as a result.

20

As DCI Culverhouse blew across the top of his mug of steaming black coffee, the phone rang.

'Culverhouse,' he said, barking into the receiver.

'Ah, Jack. The sun is shining high above the town of Mildenheath this morning, yes?' came the familiar Spanish lilt of Antonio García.

'No, it's fucking raining.'

'It is? That is a shame. I must tell you, it's very nice here. I'm walking along the beach as we speak. Must already be twenty-eight degrees.'

'Well I hope you're ringing me to tell me you've booked me a first-class ticket, otherwise you can fuck off.'

'No ticket, but some juicy information. Juicier than the juiciest orange in Sevilla. I spoke with all the local municipal police departments in southern Spain and they have no record of your wife. Not under her real name, anyway. It's possible she used a pseudonym, of course, but if she had been living in Spain for so many years she would have needed to visit a doctor at some point. Or rent a house, or buy a car. Anything which would have needed official papers. If she had spent so many years in Spain her passport would have run out while she was over here, for example. So she would have needed a new one — either a British or Spanish one. The Spanish authorities have no record of issuing a passport. The interesting thing is that they have no record of her in terms of social security details either. That means she must have gone eight and a half years without visiting a doctor, buying a car, anything.'

'Could she have used false papers?' Culverhouse asked.

'No chance. This isn't the 1970s any more, Jack. We're in the EU now. She'd have no more luck using fake papers here than she would in England. To put it simply, if she really has been living in Spain for eight and a half years, there'd be a record.'

'So what are you saying, Antonio? That you think she's lying? That she hasn't been living in Spain all that time?'

'Jack, it's not for me to cast aspersions on your good lady wife. I'm just here to give you the facts.'

Culverhouse nodded, more to himself than anything. He'd had his suspicions, but this just seemed to confirm it. He was angry, both at himself and at Helen for lying to him and wasting his time, which could have been used far more effectively right now. 'Thank you, Antonio. That's very useful. Tell me, though. How certain are you?'

'Oh, not certain at all. A police officer can never be completely certain, as you know. There are some very clever people out there. The question you must ask yourself is whether Helen is one of those people.'

That was something Culverhouse had long wondered himself. He said his goodbyes to Antonio and put the phone down. This was one of those times when he felt as though the world was moving much faster than he was. He tended to consider himself pretty adept at keeping one step ahead of the game, but right now he was starting to doubt himself. He had two unsolved murders with absolutely no leads to go on and an ex-wife who was seemingly wrong-footing him at every opportunity. He was a man who often felt isolated in his views and opinions, but now he felt completely alone.

Having a one-on-one meeting with Charles Hawes was like going to the dentist. You knew it was going to be painful, and you knew he could do whatever he wanted because no-one would be able to hear you scream. For that reason, amongst many others, Culverhouse tried to keep his visits to the Chief Constable down to a minimum.

Hawes had got particularly heavy handed and had begun to try asserting his authority even more since the government had introduced Police and Crime Commissioners in 2012. The PCCs not only regrettably brought politics into policing by being elected members of political parties but they were given powers over the Chief Constables of local forces, who had up until then been able to direct local policing without too much external interference.

The Police and Crime Commissioner who oversaw policing in Mildenheath and the county as a whole was Martin Cummings, a man with no experience of policing who'd simply had the fortune to be selected by the local Labour Party as their candidate in the first election.

Relations between Hawes and Cummings had been strained to say the least, resulting in Hawes applying much of the pressure Cummings had put on him, further down the food chain onto officers who were, in turn, junior to him. Officers like Culverhouse.

'I want to call a press conference to seek information on the murders of Keira Quinn and Lindsay Stott,' Culverhouse said, getting straight to the point.

'Right. Interesting. Are you saying there's a connection with the two deaths?' Hawes replied.

'Not necessarily, sir. In fact, I want to steer away from that possibility, publicly at least.'

'But privately?' Hawes said, leaning back in his chair and steepling his hands.

Culverhouse took a moment to think. 'Privately, I don't know.'

'I see. The problem I have, Jack, is that if there's a chance the murders are unconnected, it wouldn't be feasible to have you as the Senior Investigating Officer on both cases. It wouldn't be practical.'

'With respect, sir, I didn't say they were unconnected. I'm conscious of public reaction to announcing a multiple homicide before we're absolutely certain.' Culverhouse was trying to pick his words very carefully, knowing that his position as Senior Investigating Officer on both cases could be at risk if he said the wrong thing. It was a situation that had to be handled very delicately indeed.

'So you're hoping that someone will ring in with a golden nugget of information which'll help you find whoever killed both Keira Quinn and Lindsay Stott? That is, of course, if the same person *did* kill them both. Which you're not sure is the case anyway. Are you starting to see my dilemma, Jack?'

'Of course, sir. It's a tricky one. All I can do is assure you that I'm more than capable of managing both cases for now. Until we've found out for sure if there is a link. If there is, we'll go public,' Culverhouse said, instantly regretting having committed himself to that. 'If not — well — then it's a huge coincidence.'

'If not, Jack, I'll be parachuting someone in from a neighbouring force to take on one of the cases. I'm sure Malcolm Pope would be chomping at the bit to get stuck in.'

'I'm sure he would, sir,' Culverhouse replied through gritted teeth. 'And I'm sure the whole department would be delighted to see him.'

Hawes chuckled. 'Jack, I don't want that prick in my station any more than you do. But I've got the PCC breathing down my neck already. I'm not going to insult your intelligence with the whole "country's most underfunded police force" stuff, but as I see it we're at a crossroads here. I've got to choose a direction.'

'Give me a week,' Culverhouse said, putting his hands on the desk.

'A week? You do realise I'm being leant on after two days, don't you?'

'I know, sir. But sometimes these things can't be rushed.' Culverhouse noted the Chief Constable's raised eyebrow and continued talking before he could jump in. 'Within a week I'll know for sure whether we've got a link. Then we can move from there.'

'And what do I tell our dearly beloved, elected PCC in the meantime?' Hawes asked.

Culverhouse stood up and started to move towards the door. 'Tell him to fuck off and keep his nose out of policing.'

Culverhouse had taken the decision not to call Helen out straight away on what Antonio García had told him. His rational side — the experienced police officer within him — had told him that he needed to keep hold of the information and use it to his advantage at a later date. Striking at the optimal moment was the key weapon in the CID detective's arsenal. He was, however, being overpowered by Jack Culverhouse the wronged father.

As far as he was concerned, Helen had form. If he left it much longer to call her and tell her what he knew, she could be off starting another new life somewhere with her mobile phone — the only line of contact he had for her — thrown in the nearest bin or river.

What would she do when he told her that he knew she hadn't been in Spain for the last eight and a half years, though? Would that compel her to flee? Would she react violently? Or would she crack, open up and tell him everything — the real truth — about where she'd been since she walked out of their family home that day? That was what Jack wanted to find out.

As he pulled his mobile phone out of his pocket, he knew he was taking a huge risk. He wasn't quite sure why, but he decided to withhold his number by adding the digits *141* before Helen's number before calling it. That way, she wouldn't see who was calling. Would that make her more or less likely to answer? He didn't know, but it seemed like the right thing to do.

The familiar hum of the calling tone repeated itself four times before it stopped. Culverhouse was about to speak when he realised he'd got through to her voicemail, the recorded voice provided by the network provider telling him the person he'd called was unavailable. Four rings. Did that mean she'd hung up or was that about right for an unheard call to automatically go through to voicemail? Before he'd had a chance to work it out, the long, shrill beep told him it was time for him to leave a message.

'Uh, it's me. Listen, I know you haven't been in Spain. I have a contact there who'd looked into it and told me everything. I don't know why you lied, but I just wanted you to know that I know.' He paused while he thought of what to say next. 'I've been completely honest with you about everything and I hoped you would be with me as well. I know we aren't ever going to be best friends or anything again, but we can at least be open and honest like mature adults. I don't need the gory details and I don't want them either. I just want to see Emily,' he said, his anger rising. 'Just... Just fucking tell her I want to see her.'

He ended the call and slammed his mobile down on his desk, not bothering to check whether or not he'd cracked the screen. Right now, he didn't care.

As he buried his head in his hands, there was a knock at his office door.

'Fuck off,' he barked without lifting his head.

There was another knock. 'Guv, it's me,' said the familiar voice of DS Steve Wing.

'I said fucking fuck off.'

'I've got some news on Lindsay Stott's movements on the night she died, guv.'

Culverhouse lifted his head. 'Well what are you waiting for? Fucking come in.'

Steve did as he was told. 'Having a little "private moment", were you?' he said, winking at Culverhouse. 'Want to be careful, guv. The lads in IT are monitoring web usage. Hope you were using a private laptop.'

The icy, wordless stare from Culverhouse told Steve that he'd shot pretty wide of the mark and he changed the subject very quickly.

'I visited the local pubs to see if anyone could tell me anything about her. A couple of people seemed to recognise her. The landlord of the Spitfire said he'd barred her about six months back, which is pretty impressive. Must take a lot to get barred from that place. Woman in the Prince Albert said she recognised her but couldn't say from where. She assumed she'd probably been in at some point before, but certainly wasn't a regular.'

'Sorry, Steve,' Culverhouse said, interrupting. 'I thought you said you had some news?'

'I do,' Steve replied, grinning.

'Well would you mind hurrying the fuck up and telling me?'

'Right. Well, I went to the George and Dragon eventually. Probably should have gone there first, to be honest, seeing as it's right across the road from where she lived, but, y'know, I wanted to be sure and check everywhere else first.'

I wonder why, Culverhouse thought.

'When I went in there, the locals seemed to have known who she was straight away. Got a bit of a reputation, apparently, but they didn't seem to know anything about her life. Old Flo, the landlady, said Lindsay had spent the night chatting to a bloke down in the corner by the piano. Flo didn't recognise him, said she hadn't seen him before, but that doesn't mean much.'

'Did she get a name?' Culverhouse asked.

'Nope, nothing. All she could say is he was odd-looking. Wore a straw-coloured fedora, linen suit jacket and blue jeans. Probably about the same age as her, but she couldn't be sure.'

'A fedora? Who wears a fucking fedora to the pub? Come to think of it, who wears a fucking fedora at all?'

'Indiana Jones?' Steve replied, jokingly.

'Yeah, great. Put out a call to arrest Harrison Ford on sight. He'll probably be in the Spitfire nursing a pint of Foster's and a spliff.'

Steve ignored Culverhouse's sarcastic response. 'Or that German bloke. The one who cuts up dead bodies on the telly. The weird bloke. That Gunther von whatshisface.'

Culverhouse was silent for a few moments. 'You might actually not be so wide of the mark there, Steve.'

'How do you mean?' Steve asked, tilting his head slightly.

'Well, what if our man's a bit of a fan of the Gunther bloke? Think about it. We're potentially looking for someone with anatomical knowledge. We're not talking about a butcher here. Going around cutting up dead bodies, wearing a fedora? Doesn't take much imagination to presume we might have a crazed fan of the telly bloke.'

'Von Hagens. Gunther von Hagens. That's his name,' Steve said, suddenly remembering.

'Is he the sort of bloke who'd attract psychopathic fans?' Culverhouse asked, more of himself than anything.

'Anybody is, potentially. Nothing to say this bloke in the George and Dragon couldn't have latched onto it after seeing the programmes. Have you seen them? Got to say, guv, they're pretty good viewing. Really fascinating stuff.'

'Busman's holiday, Steve. In a word, no. What else did you find out?'

'Not a lot. Although Lindsay Stott drank in the George pretty frequently, no-one seemed to know much about her.'

Culverhouse had, by now, decided to go ahead with the press conference in order to try and gather more information on the murders of Keira Quinn and Lindsay Stott. He'd agreed to do it only on the proviso that it was to be framed as a general appeal for information on two unconnected crimes. He'd also stated that he wouldn't be taking any questions from journalists and that all speculation should be kept to a minimum, with them using only official information provided to them by the police and approved by Culverhouse himself. Cameras and audio recording equipment had been banned.

The press conference was to be held in the station's main meeting room, which went largely unused other than for press conferences or large meetings involving external bodies, such as the — thankfully rare — visits from the Independent Police Complaints Commission. As with much of policing, most 'meetings' tended to take place informally or within the private offices dotted around the building.

Culverhouse entered the room and sat down behind the long desk in front of the large free-standing banner displaying

the Mildenheath Police and county insignia as well as the telephone numbers for the 101 non-emergency service and the
force's own direct switchboard.

He nodded sagely at Chief Constable Charles Hawes to his
left and Wendy, who was seated to his right.

Thankfully for Wendy, it was the Chief Constable who had
selected who would be on the panel, not Culverhouse. Had it
been the other way round, she knew Luke Baxter would be sat
here in her place. Fortunately for her, the Chief Constable was
even less keen on Baxter than she was.

'Good morning, everyone,' Hawes said as the assembled
throng of journalists started to quieten down. 'I'm Chief
Constable Charles Hawes, and seated to my right are Detective
Chief Inspector Jack Culverhouse and Detective Sergeant
Wendy Knight, who are in charge of both investigations we
need some information on today.'

Wendy smiled at the recognition Hawes had provided her
as he handed over to Culverhouse.

'Good morning,' Culverhouse said, before starting to read
from his carefully pre-prepared notes. 'Firstly, I should point
out that we will not be taking any questions at the end of this
briefing and that all information for public release is contained
within the press release document that you'll each be issued
with on your way out later. Today we want to appeal for information on two suspicious deaths which have occurred in
Mildenheath over the past couple of weeks. I must stress that
these two incidents are completely independent and do not
form part of the same investigation. I would stress further that
any sort of speculation on the contrary will result in your particular publication being barred from all future press conferences
while I'm in charge.'

The assembled journalists began to look at one another, some of them having had no previous experience of Jack Culverhouse.

'Firstly, the death of Keira Quinn, who is believed to have died in the early hours of the thirty-first of August. Keira was thirty-six years old, divorced from her husband and lived alone in a flat in Ambassador Court. Her body was found in an alleyway off of Albert Street, some distance away from her flat. It's not known how she got there or where she was going to or from at the time. A photograph of her accompanies your press release. We particularly want to hear from anyone who knew Keira.'

Culverhouse took a swig of his water and continued. 'We also want to hear from anyone who knew Lindsay Stott, who lived in James Street and was a widow. She was forty-seven years old and died in the early hours of the seventh of September in a residential garden in Meadow Hill Lane. The owners of the property did not know Lindsay. She drank regularly in the George and Dragon pub and was seen in the company of a man wearing a straw-coloured fedora, linen suit jacket and blue denim jeans. We would very much like to speak with this man so as to eliminate him from our enquiries. Any further enquiries should be forwarded to our press office, who may or may not answer them.'

Culverhouse took another gulp of water, stood and exited the room. Behind him, he could hear Chief Constable Hawes closing the session and reminding the journalists that they should take a copy of the official press release on their way out. As far as Culverhouse was concerned, he'd done what he'd needed to do and he had no desire to be in a room full of journalists for a moment longer than he needed to.

Wendy had been in the office since six in the morning, poring over pages of potential leads with Culverhouse. They'd managed to collate some sort of rough outline of the lives of Keira Quinn and Lindsay Stott as much as they could, using only information which had been corroborated by at least two independent people. Information which had only been provided by one person was kept in a separate file until it could be verified or rejected.

It seemed that both had led remarkably uninteresting lives. Neither woman worked, although Keira Quinn's ex-husband had asserted that she'd worked as an escort or prostitute. Lindsay Stott seemed not to even have a bank account in her name, having conducted her entire life in cash. Her landlord — a private owner — didn't know what she did for a living and hadn't asked. She'd always paid him in cash and on time and he hadn't questioned it.

Wendy doubted that Lindsay had worked as a prostitute, especially as her evenings seemed to be spent in and around the vicinity of the George and Dragon pub. Had she been a prostitute she'd've almost certainly been working in the evenings and would surely not have provided her services free of charge as frequently as some of the pub's regulars had heard rumoured.

It was DC Debbie Weston who came bowling through the main door to the incident room first that morning, at a little after seven-thirty — a full hour before she usually arrived.

'Guv, I needed to see you,' she said, rummaging around in her bag, a little out of breath. 'It's probably nothing, but I've been up all night thinking about it.' She pulled a large hardback book out of her bag and thrust it at Culverhouse.

'Jack the Ripper?' he replied, looking at the cover. 'Is this news to you or something? Has it somehow managed to pass you by for the last hundred and twenty-five years?'

Debbie ignored his sarcasm. 'I've only started reading it in the last few days. I was looking through the cases of the first two murders of the canonical Ripper five — the ones which most experts agree he committed.'

'Yes, I know what canonical means, DC Weston,' Culverhouse replied.

Wendy raised her eyebrow and said nothing.

Debbie Weston continued. 'The first one, Mary Ann Nichols — or Polly, as she was known — was a heavy drinker who'd separated from her husband and started working as a prostitute. She was found in an alleyway with a bruised jaw, a deep incision to her neck and with slashes to the abdomen. The police said she wasn't killed at the scene where she was found. The second was Annie Chapman. She was also a heavy drinker, divorced from her husband who'd since died. She was found dead with her left arm across her chest, her legs raised and her throat and abdomen cut. She had a scarf or handkerchief wrapped around her neck which had probably been used as a gag. And get this, guv. She was found in the back garden of 29 Hanbury Street. Lindsay Stott was found at 29 Meadow Hill Lane.'

Wendy looked at Culverhouse. He seemed to be desperately trying to process it all.

'I'm not convinced,' he finally replied. 'The number 29 thing is a bit weird, but the rest of it doesn't strike me as odd. Do you know how many prostitutes and heavy drinkers there are in Mildenheath?'

'Alright, guv,' Debbie said. 'Then what about this? The first murder was committed on 31st August 1888. The second was on 7th September 1888. Do those dates ring a bell?'

'Of course they fucking do, but that doesn't mean anything. So they were killed on the same day as our two. That's the only similarity as far as I can see.'

'Are you serious, guv?' Wendy said, by now far more convinced it could be a possible lead than Culverhouse was. 'The deaths of Lindsay Stott and Keira Quinn look completely unconnected, right? What's to say they are totally connected, but only in the mind of the killer? If they match some sort of bizarre pattern he's trying to create, it all makes sense. If he's a copycat killer, trying to follow the canon of Jack the Ripper is just perfect. It's the ultimate murder mystery for most people.'

'Are you two shitting me?' Culverhouse barked. 'Jack the bloody Ripper? This isn't deepest, darkest, nineteenth century Whitechapel, Knight. It's sodding Mildenheath.'

'Guv, I think we should take it a bit more seriously. Look into it. See what other parallels could be drawn,' Wendy said, seeing that Debbie's bubble had clearly been burst.

'You can draw any parallels you like. You can see anything you want to see,' Culverhouse replied. 'They were all women.

They all had long hair. They were all British. They all lived in a town. They all had fannies. See? Piece of piss, this.'

'I think you're being facetious, sir,' Wendy said, firmly.

'Sir? Since when do you call me fucking sir?'

'When I'm angry at you, sir,' Wendy replied, only half-jokingly.

'Right, well "guv" is fine with me when you're not getting all pre-menstrual. Perhaps now you could both get down to some real work?'

Wendy shook her head and snorted. She could see she wasn't going to get anywhere by pushing him, but she knew exactly how to play Culverhouse.

'Come on, Debbie. We'll get the kettle on. Like good little girls.'

Wendy turned back as she reached the door and addressed her DCI. 'Sir, might I just add that if our killer seems to be recreating the Ripper murders, we should hope it's the canonical five he's following and not all of the ones which have been rumoured to be his. Because if there's more, they could have been happening for years, and anywhere across the country. And they'll be happening for a long time yet. Your call.'

As Wendy left the incident room, Culverhouse noticed that they'd left the Jack the Ripper book on the desk. He looked at the door and then back at the book.

Culverhouse was kicking himself for having told Hawes he'd know within a week whether the murders were linked or not. He hated committing himself to timeframes, knowing that most complicated CID cases were completely outside the normal realms of time. More often than not, things would be resolved when they were resolved.

He planned to try and steer the Chief Constable away from that particular line of conversation today, even though he'd been specifically called in to see him exactly six days after he'd promised him a decision within a week.

His plan to skirt around the conversation was thwarted straight away as Hawes got straight to the point once again.

'So, what are you going to do, Jack?'

'How do you mean, sir?'

'The two cases. What have you got? Are they linked or not?'

Even though he'd been expecting the question for days, Culverhouse still didn't have an answer. Saying yes would potentially spark a media frenzy and local panic, as well as increasing the pressure on him and his team to get results.

Saying no would mean that he'd be kicked off at least one of the cases and Malcolm Pope would be parachuted in to take over. Saying he still didn't know would lose him an enormous amount of face and probably result in both the media frenzy and the end of his leadership of both cases.

'I'm starting to think they might be, sir,' he finally replied. There was only one thing for it; he'd have to stand up to the media and ensure the shitstorm was kept to a minimum.

'You think they *might* be? Can you be a little more definite, perhaps?' the Chief Constable asked.

'Okay, yes, I'm now running with the assumption that they're linked.'

'I see. And can you tell me why?'

Culverhouse made a small grunting noise. He wasn't about to say *Because Debbie Weston's reading a book about Jack the Ripper and there's a couple of similarities.*

'The forensics and pathology reports seem to indicate some aspects of both deaths which are similar. The anatomical precision, both bodies being left away from their homes in places they weren't familiar with. Both women being divorced or separated, heavy drinkers, either not working or working as prostitutes.'

Chief Constable Hawes nodded, not taking his eyes off Culverhouse. 'But what's new? This is all stuff we knew within hours of the women dying. Why weren't you immediately certain of a link? What's changed?'

Culverhouse swallowed. 'In my experience, sir, I find it's always best to sit back and take an objective look. Taking an extra couple of days to be sure is always preferable to jumping the gun.'

'Are you sure the families of the victims would agree with you, Jack?'

'With respect, sir, the two victims don't have families.'

Hawes nodded silently. 'I'll leave it to you, Jack. I'll let you take the lead on this. But I'm warning you now, you don't have time to keep sitting back and taking objective looks. The PCC's not my biggest fan, nor am I his. I need results on this and — let's be frank — so do you. If Malcolm Pope gets wind of this, his secondment will go well above my head. He's about the only senior officer who's in bed with Martin Cummings. If you'll forgive the turn of phrase.'

'I've no idea what you mean, sir,' Culverhouse said, smiling sweetly. 'But don't worry. That prick Pope won't even get past reception. I'll make sure of that.'

'There's only one way you can do that, Jack. You and I both know that.'

'It's fine, sir,' Culverhouse said, rising from his seat. 'I'll sort it.'

Helen stared out of the window of her hotel room at the passing cars, most of them with only one occupant but many with more. Happy couples, young families, groups of friends. People all going about their daily lives, happy and carefree. Something Helen longed for.

Even in her darkest moments, she knew she had to do what was best for Emily. The only problem with that was that she didn't know what *was* best for Emily. After everything that had happened to the girl, how could she approach it?

She knew she couldn't keep fobbing Jack off for long, that much was true. Sooner or later he'd demand an answer or, worse, find it out for himself. She couldn't risk that. This had to be done on her terms. After so many years of being more than happy to play second fiddle to him, she'd only managed to regain her independence after leaving him. She certainly wasn't about to risk going back to square one again.

She turned the handle on the window and pushed it open as far as it would go, which wasn't far. The sounds of the outside world rushed in on a warm, humid breeze and it struck her how removed she felt from it all. It was probably the medication, she told herself, but that didn't reassure her much. This stuff was meant to be making her better, but more often than not it just numbed her and left her feeling frustrated and confused.

She'd been turning it over and over in her head ever since she'd spoken to Jack over a week ago. The longer she left it the more comfortable she felt, but the chances of Jack taking matters into his own hands would also grow day by day. It was a delicate balancing act.

He hadn't found her up until now, but then he said he hadn't been looking. Was that true? Jack was a proud man, she knew that much, but did that mean he was too proud to look or that he was too proud to have spent years in the wilderness without a clue as to what had happened? She realised she didn't know how to read him any more. Too much time had passed. Too much had changed.

Sometimes she wondered why she kept going. It would be far easier not to. Deep down, though, she knew why. She knew that it was right to keep fighting, no matter what. It was one of the rare times she was thankful for her stubbornness.

There'd been good times, undoubtedly, but the memories were fading. Memories of long walks in the park, Jack pushing Emily on the swings, buying ice creams, walking home and flaking out in front of the TV. She couldn't even be sure they were real memories. Were they just fantasies? She was sure she couldn't actually recall a time when Jack hadn't been so consumed with his work that he'd take a day off to become the family man. If he had, she wouldn't have left. Would she?

The subjectiveness of memory frustrated Helen. How much did she truly remember and how much had been warped and shaped by her anger and feelings about Jack? Had her mixed-up emotions played on the fragile nature of memory and distorted it out of all proportion? The more time that passed, the less sure she was. That was why she'd had to go back. That was why she'd had to return to Mildenheath. She needed to know. She had to justify what had happened. Deep down, she knew that.

In many ways, she had her answer. Jack hadn't changed, that much was clear. It still didn't answer everything, but it was enough to put her mind at rest for now. The upset and opening of old wounds had left its mark on her, though, and there was still some closure needed.

Not now, though. Now was not the time.

27

Jack Culverhouse, more than anybody, knew that sometimes you could just try too hard. That was why he often liked to sit in silence, eyes closed, nursing a glass of water, mug of coffee or preferably something stronger. At least he told himself that was the reason.

The investigation into the deaths of Keira Quinn and Lindsay Stott had entered what was referred to as the 'dead zone', the period after the initial discoveries, interviews and investigations and the point at which things started to go quiet. The truth was that most murder investigations were wrapped up pretty quickly following the results from forensics and speaking to family and friends. Once that phase was over and there were still no leads, it was time for the meticulous combing of bank records, previous employers, further door to door enquiries and an ever-growing mound of paperwork.

His few stolen seconds of tranquility were swiped from him when DS Frank Vine knocked on the office door and let himself in without waiting for an answer.

'The Dear Leader wants to see you in his lair,' Frank said. 'Sounds important.'

'It usually is. That's what being the Chief Constable entails, Frank.'

Frank shuffled on his feet, shrugged his shoulders and left the room. After taking a couple of moments to compose himself, Culverhouse followed.

The Chief Constable's office was situated on the top floor of Mildenheath Police Station, being both awkward to access and giving the psychological impression of Hawes being top dog — as well as the accompanying views across Mildenheath Common and beyond.

The office of the Chief Constable had once been permanently located at Mildenheath Police Station back when the town was the most prominent within the county, but most central business had since moved to plush new offices twenty miles up the road at Milton House. The vast majority of CID had gone the same way, but Mildenheath had been fortunate to retain a small CID team of its own, partly for reasons of political concession but perhaps more so due to the mechanics of supply and demand.

Hawes's office was situated at Milton House, too, but he retained one at Mildenheath for times when it would be more practical, such as when Mildenheath CID had complex or prominent cases on the go.

As Culverhouse reached the office, he knocked on the door and waited for Hawes to answer before going in.

'Ah, Jack. Do sit down. Tea? Coffee?'

'I'm fine, thanks,' Culverhouse replied, sitting in the black leather office chair nearest to him.

'How's everything going? Any progress?'

'We're always progressing, sir,' Culverhouse said. 'Perhaps not always as fast as we'd like, but you know these things take time.'

'I do. I do indeed,' Hawes replied. It was Culverhouse's saving grace that Hawes had himself come up through the CID branch of policing and knew the pressures and unexpected deviations the job brought. 'But unfortunately for us, the Police and Crime Commissioner's not quite so knowledgeable in this area.'

'What, policing?' Culverhouse asked, only half joking.

Hawes chuckled. 'I'll pretend I didn't hear that. Martin Cummings is a democratically elected official, don't you know.'

'Funnily enough, he has mentioned it once or twice. Is that what this is all about, sir? The PCC putting on pressure for results? Because I hate to say it, but this pissing about, dragging me into endless meetings for updates isn't doing anything to speed up the process. If anything, it's slowing it down. You know what I think about politicians meddling in policing, but when he's in danger of fucking up a double murder investigation it's more than a step too far.'

'Oh, I agree, Jack. I quite agree,' Hawes said, raising his hands in mock surrender. 'You're preaching to the choir on that one. But it's... different this time.'

'Different? How?' Culverhouse asked, cocking his head.

Hawes sighed loudly and stood up from his seat, moving over to the window to look out at his exclusive view over Mildenheath Common. 'We're lucky to be here, Jack. In this building, I mean. Right in the middle of a bustling town. Right on the doorstep of the people we protect and the scrotes we're out to nab. Very lucky. They shut down all the other CID departments and moved them to Milton House.'

'I know,' Culverhouse replied. He had always been thankful that Hawes had put his foot down when the government had demanded more 'streamlined' policing a few years back and had resisted what otherwise amounted to a complete takeover by county hall.

'Out in the middle of bloody nowhere. Nearest civilisation, Lower Norton: population 42. Just where you want your finest crew of detectives. I didn't have much say over that, but I was at least able to kick up as much of a fuss as I could. The Home Office weren't keen on the prospect of being taken through the courts by people who knew better than them, which is why we got certain concessions. Concessions made to me as the Chief Constable. This CID department being one. But, as you know, the system doesn't quite have the same... hierarchy any more.'

'Cummings?' Culverhouse asked, already knowing the answer to the question.

'Cummings. I'm sure you already know — we all bloody know — this is the most underfunded police force in the country. Anywhere else, that'd be hugely disappointing. With our crime rate, it's a bloody travesty. The PCC's keen to cut costs where he can, and he's not convinced that running a satellite CID office in Mildenheath is worth the money.'

'Well he can go fuck himself,' Culverhouse replied.

'Quite. But the fact remains that it's his decision. If the Home Office put pressure on him and he agrees, it happens. If he raises it himself, the Home Office will agree anyway, particularly if it's going to save them money. My opinion counts for bugger all nowadays.'

'So what, Cummings is putting the pressure on us to get results or he's going to ship us all up to Milton House to keep an eye on us?'

'Not quite, Jack. We've more or less got a full CID department here. And all the associated baggage. If he subsumes that
into Milton House, there's no way all the staff will be needed.
There'll be redundancies. And big shake-ups. You practically
run the CID show here. Do you reckon you'll get the same deal
up at county hall with Malcolm Pope in the building?'

Culverhouse didn't say a word. He didn't trust himself to.

'And that's not all,' Hawes continued. 'Cummings isn't keen
on me. Never has been. The feeling's more than mutual,
though. The only thing that keeps me from blowing up at him is
being able to come and keep an eye on things down here and get
away from him for a bit. If we had permanent offices next to
each other, I'd be out on my ear inside six weeks. He's just
looking for a reason to do it.'

'Don't give him one, then.'

'Not that easy, Jack. As you know, if someone wants to find
a reason, they'll find one.'

Hawes sat back down at his desk. Culverhouse stared at the
telephone sat next to his computer keyboard, mainly because he
didn't want to make eye contact with Hawes.

'What I'm saying, Jack, is I'm on your side here. What can I
do to help?'

Culverhouse swallowed and stood up. 'Nothing. I can
handle it.'

28

25TH SEPTEMBER

He looked at his watch. Almost three o'clock in the morning.

He'd given them too much credit. Far too much credit. He was expecting a few links to have been figured out by now. Even the Victorian bobbies had started picking up suspects by now.

The not knowing was infuriating him. Were they just playing games? Was the silence and apparent cluelessness just another police tactic to try and smoke him out? Perhaps it was the endless bureaucracy the modern day police would no doubt have to go through. Maybe that was slowing them down. Or perhaps it was just that they were fucking incompetent.

He hoped that wasn't the case. The chase wouldn't be much fun if it was. How can you run a race against a one-legged man? You can't. Maybe he'd been too clever. Perhaps his clues weren't quite obvious enough. Perhaps he needed to be more conspicuous.

It was fine. It was all fine. He'd been planning for this eventuality, or rather history had. There was a precedent at this point in time, and he was secretly quite glad he had good cause to use it. It'd be a nice touch, wouldn't it? And it'd certainly be one clue they couldn't ignore or fuck up like they had with all the others.

Because everyone would know what this meant. Even the most pig-headed doughnut-munching beat bobby would figure out what it was referring to. Anyone with any sort of interest in murder. In death.

He paced around the dark room, trying to calm his breathing. *In through the nose, out through the mouth.* Deep breaths. That's what his doctor had taught him. That was the easiest way without pills. And pills weren't an option. Not now. Doctors knew things, could tell things. He couldn't be coming face to face with a doctor now. He was great at covering things up — in so many ways — but he needed to stay under the radar.

A solitary shaft of light streamed into the room through the gap in the blinds. He'd need to get that fixed. He couldn't think in the light. He needed silence, darkness, to dull his senses and heighten his thinking. Only under cover of darkness could he truly be free.

29

Suzanne Corrigan collapsed onto her office chair and groaned as the air was pushed out from her lungs. Another day, another dollar. In any other job that old saying would probably seem quite outdated, but her salary didn't amount to a whole lot more than that as it was.

This was probably the shortest amount of time it'd taken her to become seriously jaded with a job. And she'd had some jobs. Even four months stacking shelves in Sainsbury's had seemed like a fairground ride compared to this. Growing up in Cardiff just before the city's huge regeneration scheme, she'd seen how difficult it was for her peers to get a job without leaving in a London-bound direction. It was the same struggle her parents had had thirty years earlier when they'd been forced to leave the IRA-riddled streets of Belfast for work and safety on the mainland.

She'd wanted to be a journalist for a while, and when she'd seen the opportunity advertised on her local paper she jumped at the chance. The starting pay wasn't great, but she was confident she'd move up the ladder before long. That was until she actually started the job and realised there was no ladder. Not unless you knew people or were at least willing to have sex with them.

She'd pretty quickly realised that the people above her in the pecking order were either family friends of the paper's owners or else were leggy blondes or testosterone-driven young blokes who were presumably more than happy to shag the middle-aged middle-management to get on in their careers.

Suzanne's main journalistic interest had always been in crime, which was what had originally drawn her towards the job on the Mildenheath Gazette. She'd long been fascinated by the inner machinations of the police force and read with great relish the memoirs of serving police officers from the 1980s and before, revealing the scandals and dark, murky practices of the bygone era of policing. The irony wasn't lost on her that her job reporting on the much cleaner modern day police force was being done against the backdrop of one of the seediest, most dubious industries still operating in its present form.

There were good journalists. She knew that. There were thousands of them, and she counted herself as one of them. But, like her, they were almost all on the bottom rung and destined to stay there for some time to come. Particularly if, like her, they were of a larger build than average and didn't give two hoots about caking themselves with make-up or designer clothes.

The lack of sleep didn't help. She couldn't help it, but she'd been up half the night thinking about other jobs she could do. The problem was she was thirty-two years old and had never held down a full career. She'd told the editors at the Gazette that journalism was all she'd ever wanted to do but that she'd lacked the self confidence to go for it up until now. That was mostly true, but the fact remained that she was hardly going to be a prime candidate for promotion.

She had, thankfully, been able to lose herself somewhat in the two recent murders that'd happened in the town. At least that had given her workday some meaning.

Humming a random cheerful ditty in order to try and motivate herself into believing she was actually happy to be here, she looked at the pile of incoming mail in her desk tray and instead decided to boot up her computer and tackle her email first. She opened Outlook and the computer told her she had 143 unread messages. She decided on balance to opt for the desk tray.

Most were the usual round-robin press releases from PR companies and businesses which had either yet to adapt to email or had instead deduced that being one of the few remaining people to send hard-copy releases would somehow get theirs noticed amongst the hundreds of others. There were a couple of handwritten letters from local residents who were sure their exclusive and exciting story about the scandal of the dropped kerb in their street would be sure to hit next week's front pages and, as always, a good few pieces of mail which'd been put on her desk when, really, they were nothing to do with her at all.

Then there was the handwritten letter that she held in her hand now as she began to shake and murmur the words, 'Oh God.'

30

Wendy's head was filled with a mixture of impending doom and sheer excitement as she leaned over the shoulder of DC Debbie Weston, with Culverhouse and Suzanne Corrigan crowding round the table in the incident room.

'How closely does it match up?' Wendy asked Debbie, who was thumbing through a large hardback copy of the Jack the Ripper book she'd been reading.

'Large chunks of it are word for word. Some bits are missing completely, but with good reason. The context of the original wouldn't mean anything in this case. Call it a modern day version, if you will. But there's no mistaking that whoever wrote this is referring to the original. Most of it is identical, even down to the spelling and grammar errors.'

Wendy glanced down at the letter Suzanne Corrigan had received that morning and read it again, carefully.

Dear Boss,

I keep on hearing the police are nowhere near catching me yet. I laughed at the press conference when they look so clever and talk about being on the right track. I am down on whores and I shant quit ripping them till I do get buckled. Grand work the last job was. I gave the lady no time to squeal. How can they catch me now. I love my work and want to start again. You will soon hear of me with my funny little games. The next job I do I shall clip the ladys ears off and send to the police officers just for jolly wouldn't you. Keep this letter back till I do a bit more work, then give it out straight. My knife's so nice and sharp I want to get to work right away if I get a chance. Good Luck. Yours truly

Jack the Ripper

'Look at these bits,' Debbie said. 'Word for word what was in the original. Even the missing apostrophes in "shant" and "ladys", and the grammar — "the last press conference when they look so clever". It's identical.'

'Why not the bits about the blood and the red pen?' Wendy asked.

'Maybe he only had a blue biro,' Culverhouse quipped.

'The Leather Apron stuff from the original wouldn't make any sense here, nor the mention of being a doctor. That's probably because we never mentioned that in the press conference,' Debbie said.

'What's your view then?' Culverhouse asked her. 'Seeing as you've read the book, I mean.'

'Well, he's leaving out bits that aren't pertinent to the modern day versions of the killings, as he sees them. Which I think we now have to accept is what's going on, don't you? If that's the case, the bits he's left in *are* relevant. Which means we can expect him to send us a lady's ear if we don't catch him before he gets to her. Whoever she is.'

'Fuck,' Culverhouse replied. 'We must be able to narrow it down, though. Who was the third Ripper victim?'

Debbie flicked back a few pages through the book to locate the information.

'The third victim was Elizabeth Stride, born Elisabeth Gustafsdotter in Gothenburg, Sweden. Moved to England when she was about twenty-three Five feet five inches tall. Forty-five years old when she died.'

'Married?' Culverhouse asked. 'History of prostitution?'

'She married in 1869, three years after moving to the UK. They owned a coffee shop, and apparently she claimed that her husband and children were killed in a steam ship disaster, which was later found to be a lie. Her husband died in 1884 and a year later she was living with another man. There's some evidence that she was an occasional prostitute, yes.'

'She seems to fit the type, then,' Culverhouse replied.

'What type?' Wendy replied. 'If you mean the MO of the original Ripper, then yes, but the only MO we have for the current one is that he seems to be finding people who meet some — not all — of the original victims' attributes. So if you're about to say that the next victim will be another prostitute, think again. Lindsay Stott wasn't a prostitute, for a start.'

'Only because she gave it away for free,' he snorted.

Wendy glanced sideways at Suzanne Corrigan, who was still sat at the table watching this all going on.

'Where was the letter when you received it?' Wendy asked her.

'In my desk tray, along with a load of other letters. It came in through the mail room with everything else, so it must have been through the mail system.'

'Which means it could've been posted anywhere,' Culverhouse added. 'We'll need to get forensics to analyse the paper and ink. They'll be able to tell us what type of paper and pen were used. With any luck, there'll be traces of DNA, too. Fingerprints, maybe, or a bit of hair or skin.'

'I'll get it fast tracked,' Wendy said.

Culverhouse was silent for a few moments before looked sternly at Suzanne Corrigan. 'Whatever happens, this stays completely secret, understand? I don't want to see this popping up in your paper. There'll be a time, not long, when we can make this public, but not just yet. If I promise you the exclusives, will you promise to only report on what we permit? I don't think I need to warn you about little things like contempt of court.'

'No, of course not. You have my word,' Suzanne replied, her voice quivering.

Somehow, Culverhouse knew she was telling the truth.

The emergency briefing that day had a very different tone to most other briefings. It wasn't often that the police had what essentially amounted to a pre-warning of a murder about to take place without knowing the identity of the intended victim.

Culverhouse stood up and briefed the team. 'We know that if the killer intends on following the original Ripper pattern, the next murder is likely to happen in the early hours of the twenty-ninth. That's the day after tomorrow. Now, we've got two options. We could either go public with this and panic everyone in the town and surrounding area or we can focus our energies on likely targets and release a warning nearer the time if we are no closer to identifying a target. We'll also be heavily increasing foot patrols and liaising with neighbouring forces with a view to getting some outside help on that front.

'Now, again assuming that he's following a pattern matching the original Ripper victims, we'd expect his next target to match one or more of a number of identified criteria. These are the woman's age, which could be around her mid forties, possibly of Swedish descent although any European immigrant could be at risk, divorced and possibly living with a new partner, and possibly an occasional prostitute.'

DS Frank Vine raised his hand.

'Yes, Frank?'

'Do you mean to say that we could be looking for a woman who's in her mid forties, *or* from Europe somewhere, *or* divorced, *or* working as a prostitute? Not all of them?'

'Not necessarily, no. Keira Quinn and Lindsay Stott matched some of the characteristics of Polly Nichols and Annie Chapman but certainly not all of them. It'd be impossible to find a modern day clone of all the victims, which is what makes our job all the more difficult. But I think it's fair to say that if someone matched at least two of those criteria, we'd see them as a high risk target.'

'But that could apply to hundreds of people, guv,' Steve Wing chipped in.

'Then you're going to have hundreds of fucking phone calls to make, aren't you? It's either that or this bastard kills again, and I'm not keen on that possibility.'

'Guv, there's more,' Debbie Weston said, her voice faltering slightly as she spoke, not taking her eyes off the hardback book on Jack the Ripper, which was open on her desk.

'What is it?' Culverhouse barked, by now growing impatient.

'The murder of Elizabeth Stride wasn't the only one that happened on the twenty-ninth. The Ripper killed twice that night.'

'Are you fucking kidding me?' Culverhouse shouted, trying desperately to keep a lid on his temper.

'I'm sorry, guv. I was in such a hurry to get things moving to try and stop the next one, I hadn't thought to look over the fourth again.'

'Give me the details,' Culverhouse said in his trademark gentle whisper which actually said *I'm fucking furious*.

'Her name was Catherine Eddowes. She was forty-six years old, about five feet tall, originally from Wolverhampton. Not married, but had a couple of long-term partners. Not known to be a heavy drinker, but had a bit of a temper, known to the police and had Bright's Disease, apparently.'

'What's that?' Culverhouse asked.

'Something to do with the kidneys, ain't it?' Steve Wing said.

'Thank you, Doctor Wing. Perhaps you could contribute further once you've Googled it for me,' the DCI replied. 'So we're potentially looking for someone with this Bright's Disease, then. Surely there must be some sort of society or charity who'd know about local sufferers? Maybe get onto doctors and ask them if anyone local has been diagnosed with Bright's Disease recently.'

'Ah, not likely to be much help, guv,' Wendy interrupted, holding her iPhone in the air. 'I've just Googled it. It doesn't exist any more, technically. It'd usually be described as nephritis these days.'

'Ask them if anyone's been diagnosed with fucking nephritis, then. What does the name matter? A Snickers is still a fucking Marathon.'

'We could just as easily be looking for a woman in her mid-forties who hasn't been married. Or a woman from the Midlands,' Wendy said. 'Whichever way we look at it, it's a needle in a haystack. And that's assuming that he's using the same criteria we assume he will. What if he's using something more obscure.'

'What do you suggest we do, Knight? Just sit around and wait for two more bodies to pop up?'

'I don't think getting angry's going to help anything, guv,' Wendy replied, immediately regretting it as she saw Culverhouse's face grow redder. 'If you ask me, I think your idea of stepping up foot patrols is going to be our best bet. We should warn people to be extra vigilant, too. Especially women.'

'If you ask me, it's a miracle no-one has written in linking Keira Quinn and Lindsay Stott to the original Ripper yet,' Frank Vine said.

Culverhouse replied to him without taking his eyes off Wendy. 'Yeah, well I've got a feeling that's about to be blown out the fucking water.'

They say that knowledge is power. Knowing that two women were about to be murdered certainly didn't help anyone on the investigation to feel anything but powerless, particularly as they didn't know where the killer was going to strike or who his target was. They only knew when.

The scale of the operation was unprecedented in the town, and all whilst trying to avoid panicking members of the public. Culverhouse had agreed that the public should at least be told that the police were now linking the deaths of Keira Quinn and Lindsay Stott, and that their killer might pose a danger to other women in and around Mildenheath. To that effect, women were advised not to leave the house alone and to ensure their home security was more than adequate.

Culverhouse was keen to ensure that a balance was achieved between caution and panic. Local residents needed to be aware of the dangers — they had a right to be aware of them and their caution could help the police to catch the killer — but he knew from experience that public hysteria would be counter-productive.

The Chief Constable had agreed that patrols in the town needed to be stepped up. As the most underfunded police force in the country, they couldn't rightfully pull numbers of police officers from other areas of the county, and the decision had instead been taken to halt and rescind all booked holidays and off-days. All police officers assigned to the county's force would be required to report for duty immediately, provided they weren't breaching health and safety laws on working hours.

Uniformed PCs had also been drafted in from neighbouring forces, with the increased numbers being used to form foot and vehicle patrols in and around Mildenheath. The intention was not only to reassure the public but to use the vastly increased police presence to try and scupper the Ripper's plans. Knight and Culverhouse knew from experience that killers tended to make mistakes when they were forced to change their carefully-laid plans. And when killers made mistakes, they were caught.

A list of potential victims had been drawn up, but it contained almost three hundred possibilities from the Police National Computer alone. Based on people living within ten miles of Mildenheath town centre, that was the number of potential targets indicated by looking at middle-aged women of Scandinavian or North European origin, or women who were known to be born in the Wolverhampton area, or women of non-British European origin who were known to be working as prostitutes in and around the town.

With a list so large, it would be impossible to keep tabs on them all or even to warn half of them of the potential danger. As the list came from the PNC, it only contained people who were already known to the police. If the Ripper's next two victims had never been arrested, they'd have no record of them at all and no way of warning them of the potential danger to their lives.

It had been proposed that temporary roadblocks could be set up on the roads into and out of Mildenheath, but this was decided to be impractical. There were eight main routes which could be used to access the town — far more if you included the surrounding estates and spillover areas. What's more, there was nothing at all to say that the killer was coming from outside Mildenheath. Both murders to date had been of local women, found dead in the town and presumably killed somewhere in the town too. A temporary roadblock would be hugely expensive and probably fruitless.

Watches were being put on local doctors — particularly those who lived in the town — and a shortlist of twenty-five GPs and hospital doctors with extensive surgical knowledge working in the town had been drawn up. Three firms of private detectives, mostly consisting of ex-police officers, had been hired to watch the homes and workplaces of these doctors for twenty-four hours.

The financial cost of the operation was huge, but its saving grace was that it would only be necessary for twenty-four hours. The force's psychological profiler, Patrick Sharp, had told the incident room that he believed the killer would stick rigorously to his pattern. His modus operandi depended heavily on mirroring the events of 1888 and he'd not deviate from something as seemingly important as the dates of the murders. He'd stuck remarkably closely to the original Ripper's MO up until now and Sharp didn't think he had any intention of changing that now.

For Wendy, the sick feeling in the pit of her stomach was

almost unmanageable. It was not a position she was used to, knowing that two innocent women were about to be killed but knowing deep down that she would be unable to do very much about it at all.

33

29TH SEPTEMBER

They'd tried their best, he was sure of that. But he was even more sure that there was no way they were going to stop him doing what he'd always intended to do. Because, after all, he was one step ahead. He had been all along.

Why did they think he'd sent the letter to that fat bitch journalist? Because it was pretty fucking clear they didn't have two brain cells to rub between them and work out the link between him and the Ripper. He'd given it to them on a plate and they'd taken it hook, line and sinker.

He knew exactly what they'd be looking for. He knew because he'd practically told them to do it. He'd been careful from the start, sticking to his plan but ensuring that they'd never be able to pre-empt him. That was his job. The story needed to be finished. The canon needed to be completed, and no-one was going to stop him doing that.

Even an entire police force panicking for twenty-four hours was not going to scupper his plans. The plans he'd been laying down for years, carefully selecting his five — plus the all-important back-up lists, planning the locations and the methods.

He knew this town like the back of his hand. He knew its people. He knew its places. He knew, for example, that the Vincents on Meadow Hill Lane always left their gate unlocked. He'd spent an enormous amount of time scouring the town on Google Maps for a number 29 which even had a gate and large garden like that one. How he'd hit the jackpot when he found it! The three weeks of walking past each night and trying the gate to make sure it was unlocked were well worth it.

So far, that had been the trickiest part of his plan to execute. Forming his list of five — and the backups — hadn't been difficult at all. It was just a matter of time, waiting for them to come to him.

He knew his point was being proven — he knew the modern police force was not much more advanced than the Victorian one — but he would not have put money on them being worse. He hadn't gambled on his having to help them out as much as he had done.

He smiled and chuckled to himself as he considered this, feeling very proud of himself. As he did so, the woman murmured and started to move.

'Now, now,' he said, putting a reassuring hand on her shoulder as she struggled against the silver tape that'd been used to bind her arms and legs as well as being placed over her mouth to stop her screaming. 'You're not going to be heard here, so I wouldn't try that. You can squirm all you like. Adrenaline's known to numb pain, but I must warn you that too much movement means the cuts won't be so clean. They might actually hurt more.' He smiled as he tied the handkerchief around her neck — not too tight.

The woman's eyes were bloodshot, panicked, the tears streaming down her face as the man unsheathed his scalpel and brought it across her oesophagus. The woman started gurgling and wheezing through the new hole in her neck as her lungs pooled with blood.

'You're number three. That's what they'll call you. Of course, I wouldn't be so callous. You'll always be my Emma. The one they tried, so hard, to stop. The one who acquiesced so beautifully despite it all. I'll always remember that.'

The words rang tinnily in her ears as death took her.

34

Barely ten seconds after answering the call, Culverhouse was in the car, Wendy beside him, racing up the high street.

'The working men's club next to the car garage,' he said as he switched on the siren and sped through a set of red lights. 'A patrol officer found her behind a bin in the car park. Poor bastard's blaming himself, apparently. Says she's still warm.'

'Christ. Any ID?'

'Yep, positive, apparently but we'll find all that out when we get there. How the fuck did he manage it, though? With all the patrols we've got out and about. It's right on the fucking high street, barely two hours after closing time. The staff probably hadn't even been gone long. He's getting fucking brave, that's for sure.'

Foremost in Wendy's mind was that this meant another murder was due to occur somewhere in the town within the next couple of hours. The news had already been relayed to the patrol officers, ensuring that they knew they had to be on top of their game and on the highest state of alert with regards to lone males or females in the town.

As they parked up in the entrance road to the working men's club, Wendy jumped out of the car and jogged round to the rear car park, where three uniformed officers were already waiting.

'Anybody touched anything?'

'Nothing, sarge,' said one of the officers while the other two shook their heads.

'Who found her?'

'PC Rashid. He's round there, honking up,' the officer said, pointing towards the door which Wendy presumed went straight into the working men's club's kitchen.

'Lovely. Dr Grey should be here soon. Funnily enough, she was kind of expecting a call right about now. Don't touch anything until she gets here.'

Wendy could see that even though the woman's skin still held the colour of life, she was clearly not about to take another breath. By now, Culverhouse had caught up and was speaking to the two shocked, silent PCs.

The woman was lying facing the wall of the car park, her legs drawn up and her throat cut — this was clearly visible even through the now-familiar handkerchief that was tied around her neck. As she noted this, her earpiece crackled as the radio buzzed into life. It was the control room.

'We've had a call from an anonymous male in a phone box who's reported a woman's body behind the working men's club on the high street. Could nearby officers please attend?'

Wendy pressed the button on her radio and spoke back. 'I'm about six inches away, will that help?'

'Who the fuck called that in?' Culverhouse barked. 'There's no phone box around here, is there?'

'Not that I know of,' Wendy said, pressing the button again

to speak to the controller. 'Can you get a trace on the phone box please?'

'Guv, you seen this?' one of the PCs said, gesturing to a large hole which had been cut in the chicken wire fence at the other side of the car park. 'Looks like it's fairly recently cut. Isn't rusted or anything.'

'Where does that go?' Culverhouse asked.

'Lawn bowls club on Sycamore Close. Just off Meadow Hill Lane. The road's probably six or seven hundred feet away.'

'And it's a much fucking quieter road than the high street,' Culverhouse replied. 'Get the fence tested for DNA. Any hair, fibres from clothing or even blood from the victim. If he's come in or out that way, he could be anywhere by now.'

Wendy's radio buzzed in her ear again. 'Got that trace, sarge. The call was made from the phone box on Allerdale Road, next to the church. The caller sounded very calm, apparently. Almost matter-of-fact.'

'Jesus. Allerdale Road? Right, find out if there's any CCTV anywhere nearby. There's a row of shops right near that. One of them must have CCTV outside.'

'That could be good news, sarge,' one of the uniformed PCs said.

'Please do tell me how,' Wendy replied, almost sarcastically.

'Well, if he's got up to Allerdale Road from here, through that fence, he would've had to cross Meadow Hill Lane, go up Copeland Avenue and round the back of the shops. Would've only taken five minutes at the most, if he wasn't walking quickly. Would keep him well away from most of the patrols, too. If you ask me, it looks as if our man's on foot.'

35

The chase was intense. He knew exactly where they'd be going and when. He knew because he'd practically planned it for them.

He knew, for instance, that they would've traced his call to the phone box on Allerdale Road. He also knew that they'd know from the tone of his voice that he wasn't just a random passer-by who'd discovered a dead body by complete chance. They'd know it was him. They'd also know that to get to Allerdale Road in time, he would've had to have gone by foot, through the hole in the fence by the bowls club. The most exciting thing about it was that he wasn't trying to wrong-foot them; he was helping them out as the chase just wouldn't be the same if they were running around in circles like headless chickens.

After making the call, he'd headed straight down Colby Gardens, an adjacent road which he knew had plenty of houses with low walls, cars parked on drives and other places he could hide quickly if needed. He'd only had one car come down the road, and he'd ducked behind what looked from its shape like a classic American car, which was up on bricks and covered by a tarpaulin. The passing car was a Toyota Yaris — clearly not a police car, but he couldn't afford to be anything less than completely cautious.

He knew where most of the town's CCTV coverage was, and he knew the best route to take to avoid it. He now had to get to Alexandra Square, a small outdoor shopping precinct, which was the location for his next body. Fortunately for him, he'd already done most of the spadework. It was a case of having to, knowing that the police would be hot on his tail after the last one, knowing that he'd be due to kill again before the sun rose.

The trick was to avoid commercial premises. These were the ones which were most likely to have CCTV cameras on the front of them. These days, plenty of houses did too, although his route was taking him past areas which had far fewer than anywhere else. Oddly, the CCTV coverage in Alexandra Square was minimal. There were three entrances into the square, and only one had CCTV coverage — mainly due to the nightclub on the corner which had seen its fair share of late-night trouble spilling out into the square over the years. His route would keep him well away from the eagle-eye lens and ensure that he'd get away easily enough afterwards, too.

He'd taken great care to disguise himself, too, although that wouldn't matter in the long run. Once he'd completed his canon, it was up to them to find him in their own good time. If they managed it inside a hundred and thirty years they'd be one up on the Victorian Whitechapel police.

His pace was quick, but not so quick as to attract attention. Just quick enough to be sure that no-one was going to be suddenly gaining behind him, allowing him instead to concentrate on looking forward, giving him plenty of time to duck away should someone appear in the distance.

The walk was just under a mile in total. He estimated it'd take him sixteen minutes. His advantage was that nobody knew where he was going. They'd have officers in the vicinity, and he'd heard the cars heading towards the phone box, but, as he'd predicted, they were using Allerdale Road, Meadow Hill Lane and the other rat runs. The quiet, unassuming residential streets that ran alongside were perfectly safe in comparison.

He waited quietly at the corner of Colby Gardens in order to try and ascertain the direction of the sirens and car engine noises. He needed to cross the next road, walk about twenty yards further down and disappear down Peter's Street, a road which would take him the next step towards Alexandra Square and consisted entirely of houses with low front walls — perfect for diving behind.

Then it was down past the old folks' home and through the winding alleyway which would take him out perilously close to the police station. The wait on the next corner was longer, seeing as he had to cross the main road that passed right across the high street a hundred yards or so further down — the busy crossroads that defined Mildenheath. A lone person seen walking the streets tonight would be apprehended without fail, and this particular area was by far the most likely place for it to happen.

He took a deep breath and stood up from behind the parked car he'd been crouched behind. He marched across the road, not bothering to look — he'd already done that from his hiding place — his heart thumping in his chest as he walked quickly and quietly, keeping away from the road, before ducking down

Albert Street, where he exhaled and allowed himself to start breathing again.

A quick right turn and he was on Ship Street, just mere seconds away from his next site. He'd made it here unscathed, and he allowed himself a faint smirk as he approached the place he'd been hiding number four for the past few hours.

As he neared Alexandra Square, he noticed a young, fresh-faced police constable in full uniform, his fluorescent jacket glowing under the street light in the car park. He held his breath and ducked inside the entranceway to a block of flats, the low wall allowing him to crouch and peer around the edge. The copper was heading off in the direction of the main road he'd just crossed. A few seconds longer and he'd be able to get to the site and do what he needed to do.

He'd need to be quick. That much he knew. The copper must've literally walked right across his site only seconds earlier, and he'd be sure to come back again at some point soon. Time was of the essence if he was to stick to his plan.

Less than a minute later, he'd opened the door and peered in at the face of his next victim.

'Ah, Marla. Thank you for waiting for me. Very kind.'

36

'It's fucking brutal,' the PC said, visibly shaking as the tears rolled down his cheeks. 'I never seen a body before. Not like this.'

Wendy placed a reassuring hand on the young constable's shoulder. He'd radioed in a few minutes earlier to report the body, which he'd found on his routine patrol that night.

'I can't understand it. I only walked past ten, fifteen minutes earlier and there was nothing. I didn't see no people, no cars, nothing! I just don't get it.' The officer seemed almost inconsolable.

'There's no use beating yourself up about it,' Wendy said. 'This guy's something else. He was probably watching you the whole time, waiting for the right moment.'

'I should've seen him!'

'No-one saw him. Do you have any idea how many officers are out on the streets tonight? We knew he was going to kill, we even knew when, but no-one managed to stop him. You can't take it personally.'

'I just can't believe it. We always knew the fourth victim

would be killed in some sort of square. Like the original. Why wasn't there more officers in the squares?'

'There was,' Wendy replied. 'Granted, we focussed on the main square by the clock tower, and the Courtyard, but we had no way of knowing what he thought constituted a square. There are ten roads alone in the town called "Square". There wasn't anything else we could've done. All the main shopping areas had extra officers. You were one of them.'

Wendy realised from the resultant look on the young officer's face that that last comment hadn't helped much.

'She's not been dead long. Certainly the same chap who did it, as if you didn't already know,' Dr Janet Grey said from her position kneeling over the body. 'Similar MO. On her back, one of her legs bent up. Not to mention the throat being cut.'

'I suppose you've also noticed that her fucking innards have been ripped out and thrown over her shoulder?' Culverhouse interrupted.

'I did notice that, yes. How very observant of you, Jack,' Dr Grey retorted. 'That's not something we've seen before, but I can't say it was unexpected. That's what happened to Catherine Eddowes back in 1888, too.'

'How the fuck did he do it, though? I mean, getting a woman here kicking and screaming in the middle of the biggest manhunt in the county's history. How did he manage that?'

'She might not have been kicking and screaming,' the pathologist replied. 'I won't know until we've got the toxicology results back. If you ask me, the sensible option would've been to have drugged her unconscious and had her somewhere nearby, ready to finish the job.'

'The sensible option would've been not to have bothered at all,' Culverhouse replied.

'Can't argue with that. There is one saving grace, though, Jack,' Dr Grey said, standing and removing her blue latex gloves.

'If this is some sick pathology joke, you can fuck off,' Culverhouse replied.

'Not at all. I was just thinking, if I remember correctly, the fifth Ripper victim was killed on the ninth of November. That gives you, what, six weeks to stop him this time, if that helps.'

'Oh yeah. That's great,' he said. 'Just fucking great.'

37

The incident room was eerily quiet that morning, a mixture of tiredness at most of the officers having been up all night and the anguish at having been bettered — twice — by what they had already begun referring to as the Mildenheath Ripper.

Culverhouse's main worry was that there was no way he was going to be able to head the press off after this. The heavy police presence in the town hadn't gone unnoticed, but it didn't seem to have sparked panic. Suzanne Corrigan had been persuaded not to run any stories involving mentions of the Ripper up until now, and the team had been very careful not to make details of the last two killings known to anyone outside the force. But he knew it would be nigh-on impossible for it to remain that way.

All in all, that meant that Mildenheath would be on the verge of public hysteria. A serial killer never went down particularly well anywhere, but in a town like Mildenheath, it would go down about as well as a skid mark on a hired wedding suit.

He would have to speak with Suzanne Corrigan. The details of the killings simply could not be leaked, else some canny member of the public would piece things together inside twenty seconds and the announcement that another murder was due on the ninth of November would be all over the town within minutes. Come that date, there'd be people out on the street with burning lanterns and pitchforks, which wasn't what anyone wanted.

'Needless to say, the link between the original Ripper killings and what's been happening in Mildenheath over the past few weeks is now pretty indisputable,' Culverhouse said to the assembled officers. 'It seems that the Ripper is now following the canonical five, which means that we're looking at one final victim, due to die on the ninth of November.' As he said this, he realised how bizarre it sounded. It was six weeks away, and already he was predicting the death. 'Debbie?'

DC Debbie Weston stood and made her way to the front of the room as Culverhouse sat down. 'The fifth Ripper victim was Mary Jane Kelly,' she said, holding up a contemporary sketch of the woman. 'There are a number of notable aspects about her which might lead us to identifying the modern day equivalent in our Ripper's mind. We've got a much longer timeframe this time. Mary Jane Kelly was born in Ireland but moved to Wales as a child and spoke fluent Welsh. She got married at sixteen and her husband was killed in a coal mine explosion a couple of years later. Some sources say they had a child, but others say they didn't. Apparently, she worked as a prostitute in Cardiff,' Debbie said, before Culverhouse interrupted her.

'Well there's a fucking surprise. What is it with serial killers and prostitutes around here? I'm surprised there's any of the fuckers left after the nut jobs have finished their killing sprees.'

Wendy shot him a look.

'Your brother excepted, of course,' Culverhouse added.

'My brother is a monster. I know that much, guv.'

'Yes. Well. At least now we know he's not alone in his particular penchant, don't we?'

Debbie Weston duly noted the awkward silence and continued. 'Mary Jane Kelly moved to London in 1884, which was four years before she was killed. That might be pertinent to our Ripper's fifth intended victim, too. There are records of people saying she was violent and abusive when drunk, but fine when sober.'

'Well that narrows it down, doesn't it?' Culverhouse interjected. 'Might as well warn every old trollop propping up the bars in every pub in town. That'll take most of our six weeks.'

'We've got a fair bit to be running with,' Debbie replied. 'The Irish and Welsh connection, possibly fairly new to the area, potentially working as a prostitute or escort, married young and widowed early. We should be able to draw a fairly narrow shortlist.'

'Starting with what?' Frank Vine butted in. 'The PNC? Only any use if she's known to us. If she's moved here within the last four years or so she won't be on the census. We can't just put a big sign in the town centre saying "Irish and Welsh hookers with dead husbands, call us now."'

'I think we can afford to be a little more tactful than that,' Culverhouse said, the irony of his comment completely lost on him. 'We've got six weeks, potentially. If we have to knock on every door in the town, we will. It can be done. Our killer seems to be fairly well connected to the social scene. He knows people's backgrounds. We're potentially looking at someone in a position of trust, but still with an anatomical or medical background. I'm thinking doctors, surgeons, potentially dentists.'

'Pub landlords?' Steve Wing added.

'How many pub landlord do you know with advanced anatomical knowledge, Steve?'

'Well, not many, but there must be some who went through medical school. Or who've read up on it. What I mean is they'd be in a position to know people's lives and backgrounds. And their habits. We know that at least two of our victims regularly drank in local pubs. Hairdressers hear quite a lot about people's lives, too. They work with scissors and knives and stuff.'

'Steve, I...' Culverhouse started to talk but quickly realised there was no point. 'I think we need to look at all GPs working in the area for a start. He obviously knows people from the town and their life stories and histories, so it's unlikely to be a doctor living locally who works elsewhere. Far more likely the other way round. Surgeons are probably less likely in terms of hearing people's life stories. Perhaps we also need to look at counsellors. Especially ones with medical knowledge. I don't think there's any record of our victims all visiting a counsellor, though. Get onto that one for me, Luke,' he said, pointing at Baxter. 'I want to see records on all four victims to date. I need to know their GPs, any medical history of doctors they've seen in the past ten years. It's likely our man's been planning this for a while. I also want to know their hairdresser, the pubs they drink in — everything that might connect them to someone who'd know all about their lives. That way we might find a link.'

38

After making two mugs of strong coffee — one to gulp down immediately and one to sip after — Wendy spent the evening going through the various reports she'd been handed. The first was from the officer who'd listened to the 999 call reporting the third body. It seemed as though the voice had somehow been distorted or made deliberately deep, which made it practically impossible to identify. The accent was a local one, which wasn't all that surprising, but it still couldn't be ruled out that it was being put on.

CCTV in the area had been checked, but there wasn't anything found. The cameras on the front of the shops showed nothing, and the one which covered the stairs to the upstairs flats over the shops didn't have anything on it either, which told Wendy that the caller had crossed the road earlier to walk up to the phone box. Had he done this deliberately to avoid the cameras?

Wendy had almost lost her temper when the council had told her that there were no CCTV cameras in the Alexandra Square area other than one covering the doorway of - and alleyway to - the nightclub on the corner of Alexandra Square and the High Street. Of course, it wasn't possible to cover every single inch of the town with CCTV but what disturbed Wendy was that it seemed their killer had taken great care in discovering where the cameras were and working out a route which would avoid them all. A fourth time.

DNA results from the first two bodies had shown no trace of any DNA in the database. They'd been unable to trace anything which was clearly from the killer, which showed his victims had not put up much of a fight. There was no skin or fibres under any of their fingernails, which was particularly rare and was only ever really seen when the victim trusted their killer or knew them very well. What had been discovered, though, was dust from latex gloves. This had also been found on the two most recent bodies, but DNA results wouldn't be ready for a little while yet.

She'd also been provided with more information about the lives of Emma Roche and Marla Collingwood. Their nexts of kin had been traced and interviewed, and subsequently all confirmed as not being suspects. Marla had been born in Cannock — not a million miles from Wolverhampton at all — and had been a fairly heavy drinker. She'd apparently had kidney stones a few months back but nothing more serious than that, and certainly nothing that would be the modern day equivalent of Bright's Disease.

Emma, on the other hand, had been born in Sweden as Emma Lundstromm. She moved over with her parents at a young age and had been married but separated. Her husband had apparently been very keen to help with the investigation where he could, as he and Emma had parted on good terms, but he now lived back in Ireland, where he had been born, having moved to England for work at the age of twenty.

All of these pieces of information seemed to tie up with their Victorian counterparts in at least some ways, which, in Wendy's mind, further backed up the theory that they had a Ripper copycat on their hands.

39

30TH SEPTEMBER

The bloody fools. They'd done exactly as he'd predicted they would. In a way, he'd also hoped they wouldn't. The chase was really rather boring when the chasers were so inept.

What was he meant to do? Hand it to them on a plate? The thought did appeal to him. He certainly wasn't willing to be caught by doing something stupid like walking past a CCTV camera undisguised or being recognised by somebody. No, they'd have to use their brains for once; not rely on science and technology to do the work for them. That's all the Whitechapel police had had to work with, and it had still eluded them.

If there was to be any hope for the future of public safety and human development, he was going to have to see some sign of progress very soon. After all, it was over a hundred and twenty years on from the original investigation and it seemed that nothing much had changed.

The rush of adrenaline between the third and fourth had been immense, but that was only because he'd stepped up the game and practically led them to him. He knew the way they thought, the way they reacted. That wasn't going to make him stop taking advantage of that, though. That was all part of the game. That was all part of using *their* brains to get one step ahead of *him*. This was a battle of wills.

Their next move would be interesting. It would tell him a lot, whatever they chose to do. They'd probably keep fairly quiet for a while. You'd want to, wouldn't you, if you'd just failed to stop someone killing two women, having known in advance that he was going to do it at that time and in that place. It's not something you'd shout from the rooftops about.

When the ninth of November started to creep up on them, though, he knew they'd start to panic. They'd need to step up the effort, bring in more experts and ultimately go public to do all they could to prevent the fifth and final killing. He credited them with having already worked out that he was aiming for the canonical five. If they had half an ounce of sense they'd've worked out the rest of the plan, too. They'd have realised that he'd then slip back under his cover of darkness and they'd never stand a chance of catching him.

He hated to do it, but it gave him a perverse sense of pleasure and self importance. He slipped on his latex gloves, removed the writing pad from its protective pouch and started to write.

40

Patrick Sharp looked as pumped as Wendy had imagined he might. As the force's psychological profiler, he couldn't have hoped for a juicier case to work on. The original Jack the Ripper case had eluded detectives — both professional and armchair — and psychological profilers for almost a hundred and thirty years. Copycat killers were always a particularly unique breed of serial killer, and the fact that someone in Mildenheath seemed to be replicating the Jack the Ripper killings with almost uncanny similarity was something that Patrick Sharp found both worrying and extremely exciting.

'The killer is keeping remarkably close to the original killings,' he said to a packed incident room. 'It might not seem it in many ways, but we have to remember that the original murders were almost a hundred and thirty years ago, so much of it can't be replicated these days. Even in Whitechapel itself, it'd be impossible as most of the streets and buildings don't exist any more. The question, then, has to be why Mildenheath? My own presumption would be that the killer has a close connection with the local area and its people, and probably lives in the town himself. He seems to know the area very well and managed to elude the police twice on the night of the twenty-eighth and twenty-ninth of September.'

The assembled officers exchanged a few looks, as if they didn't need reminding.

Patrick Sharp continued in his faded but still noticeable Irish brogue. 'The most worrying thing, but also the most promising in terms of narrowing the search, is how methodical and specific he is. The murders always occur on the same date as the original Ripper killings, in a place which somehow resembles the original and the victim always resembles the original, too. Not always in an obvious way, but there are always strong links. This means he must have been planning this for quite some time. I'd say probably years, with this being the first year that he'd managed to complete his canon and plan where, how and when he'd do it. He must've known the women would all be in a certain place on those dates. That's what baffles me. The alternative is that he had more than one person in mind to play the part of each victim. I find that more likely, personally.'

'What should we be looking for?' Culverhouse asked, somewhat annoyed at having things he already knew or had worked out for himself being reiterated.

'Someone with community connections. Someone who's calm and methodical. A careful planner who's happy to wait quite some time — years — to get all his pieces lined up before he even considers making his first move. That means he's probably planned absolutely everything, including the police's reactions and movements. His call from the phone box was quite likely part of that, especially considering the fact that he didn't call in any of his other murders. As much as I hate to say it, I think he successfully managed to con you with sleight of hand, there.'

Culverhouse shot him a look which said that he didn't particularly want reminding of that.

'It's the choice of location which particularly interests me. He always finds a place which somehow resembles the original location where the bodies were found. Mary or Polly Nichols was found in a gateway-cum-alleyway, as was Keira Quinn. Annie Chapman was found in the back garden of 29 Hanbury Street, Whitechapel; Lindsay Stott was found in the back garden of 29 Meadow Hill Lane, Mildenheath. Elizabeth Stride was found in a yard by a working men's club; Emma Roche was found in the car park behind a working men's club. Catherine Eddowes was found in Mitre Square; Marla Collingwood was found in Alexandra Square. Mary Kelly, on the other hand — the fifth victim — was found in her bedroom in Miller's Court in Whitechapel. You might want to look into roads or areas called Court, here, to see if there's something which might match up but it's worth opening the net on this one. It may be that the location of killing her in her bedroom is enough for him. I wouldn't discount the possibility that he's going to bring things right up close to home for himself with the last victim. With victim number four we focused on the two main squares and roads called Square in Mildenheath and neglected the tiny Alexandra Square shopping precinct. We don't want to make that mistake again.'

'Do you think perhaps you could stop going on about that?' Culverhouse barked. 'We fucked up. We know that. Perhaps if you'd actually given us something useful a bit earlier, we'd—'

'I think what Detective Chief Inspector Culverhouse is trying to say,' Wendy interjected, 'is that most of us on the team are still quite raw about what happened the other night. We don't want to make that mistake again, so we're grateful for any help you can give us.'

'Right,' Patrick Sharp said, shuffling his feet and swallowing hard. 'Well we need to look at why he's doing this. If he's of the serial killer mindset, why has he taken so much time to plan these particular murders based around the original Ripper killings? To me, it seems that he has some sort of affinity with the original case. It's possible that he feels he has a connection with one of the original suspects, or perhaps is even a descendant of one of them.'

Culverhouse's ears pricked up. 'Frank, note that down. I want you to run through the list of the original Ripper suspects and trace their family trees. See if they've got any living descendants in this area.'

Frank Vine nodded and jotted a note down on his pad. It'd be a big task, but Frank would be far happier doing this than being on the door-to-door team or marching around the town trying to 'raise awareness'.

'I think it likely that he perhaps considers one of the original suspects to have been wrongly accused,' the profiler continued. 'It's likely that our man has some sort of personality disorder. This, combined with the realisation of some — perhaps tenuous — link between him and one of the suspects could flick a switch. Importantly, he seems to be treating it all as some sort of game. A very carefully planned game. We're looking for someone with the real mind of a serial killer, not just someone who's mentally unstable and wants to kill. Another avenue worth looking at is the possibility that it's someone who thinks he's worked out who committed the original Ripper killings and is so convinced of it that he's recreating them in the hope of "proving" someone's guilt in the original killings.'

'Guv, there are hundreds of websites online about the Ripper killings,' Debbie Weston said. 'All sorts of web forums and Facebook groups where people put forward their own theories and try to "prove" that certain people could or could not have done it. It might be worth looking there for starters, but it'd be impossible to narrow it down any further. The whole subject of Ripperology is massive online.'

'Ripperology?' Culverhouse asked. 'Christ. When I was a lad, scientists used to study cancer and environmental change.'

'It's a big subject,' Debbie replied. 'People dedicate their lives to trying to prove things one way or the other when it comes to the Ripper. It's a huge money business if you can make a breakthrough. There are so many books and websites on it, it's incredible. Every time someone writes a book claiming to have proved something one way or the other, they make a mint.'

'Looks like I'm in the wrong job,' Culverhouse said. 'All I get's a pat on the back and a chocolate biscuit from the Chief Constable.'

The assembled officers allowed themselves a small laugh, which helped to break the tension.

'That's a fair bit for us to be going on,' Culverhouse said. 'Thanks, Patrick.'

'No problem. I know you're not going to like me saying this, Jack,' Patrick Sharp summarised, 'but I think you're going to have quite a job on your hands.'

41

After Patrick Sharp had left, Culverhouse declared that he thought it would be a good idea to generate a list of potential suspects based on the suspects in the original Ripper case. If the modern day Ripper was somehow emulating the murders in order to avenge a Victorian suspect or prove somebody's guilt, this seemed a particularly good place to start.

Debbie Weston had by now become the de facto incident room expert on the original Ripper killings, and it was Debbie who addressed the room with regards to the original Ripper suspects.

'The strange thing about the original case is that there still isn't an overwhelming favourite in terms of suspects. There are three or four who are considered most likely, but they all have their drawbacks. One of the prime suspects was a man called Montague John Druitt, who was a barrister and assistant schoolmaster. The only real reason he was linked to the killings was because he killed himself on New Year's Eve in 1888. There are rumours that he was gay, which led to him being sacked as assistant schoolmaster and killing himself. There are also suggestions of mental illness in the family. He had pretty strong alibis for a couple of the killings, so these days he's considered unlikely. His name is still synonymous with the Ripper killings, though, so it might well be that someone wanted to clear his name for once and for all.'

'I still don't see how killing four women somehow clears the name of a bloke from the Victorian era of five totally separate murders,' Culverhouse said.

'All psychological, guv,' Frank Vine offered.

'Helpful, Frank, thanks.'

Debbie Weston continued. 'A Polish man called Seweryn Klosowski, who later changed his name to George Chapman. He came to the UK just before the murders started, and was hanged in 1903 for poisoning three of his wives. And get this — he worked as a barber.'

'Sounds promising,' Culverhouse said.

'The police at the time dismissed him because of the different MO. His wives were poisoned using a compound called tartar-emetic. But there does seem to be a Polish link. The suspicion of an unnamed Polish man appears quite a bit in police reports at the time. That leads me on to another Polish guy, a Jewish man called Aaron Kosminski. Interestingly, there was a book out a short while back which named Kosminski categorically as being the killer. Using DNA evidence, apparently. He worked as a hairdresser and was admitted into an asylum in 1891. An interesting little nugget is that some people believe he was confused with another Polish Jew of a similar age, probably Aaron Cohen, who was in the same asylum but was reported to have heavily violent tendencies, whereas Kosminski apparently was far more gentle.'

'Another hairdresser,' Wendy remarked. 'Someone who'd be in a position to know all about people's lives and goings on.'

'And pretty handy with a sharp implement, too,' Culverhouse added. 'What's to say our girls' throats weren't cut with a razor blade?'

'We won't know until Janet Grey files her final report,' Wendy replied. 'Off the record, she reckons it's possible but she can't say for certain what was used yet.'

'They're usually considered to be the main three suspects,' Debbie continued. 'The other one which pops up quite a lot is Francis Tumblety, who was a quack doctor from America who escaped prison after a patient died following his treatment and came to England. It's said he despised women and particularly hated prostitutes. Rumour has it that he was married to a prostitute and it didn't work out.'

'Surprise surprise,' Culverhouse murmured.

'Oddly, he was arrested in 1865 for being somehow involved in the assassination of Abraham Lincoln. He fled the country within days of the fifth murder — some think perhaps even before it occurred — but these days people generally have discounted him as a suspect. He didn't match any of the eyewitness accounts and he was noted as being very tall and with an enormous moustache, which would've made him stand out, to say the least.'

'Quite possible that a modern day doctor might be trying to exonerate him, though?' Culverhouse asked.

'It's possible. Worth looking into, I'd say,' Debbie replied, beaming inside at the responsibility she was being given in this case. 'There were literally hundreds of suspects named, but other ones worth looking into would be Michael Ostrog, a Russian con man; John Pizer, a Polish Jew with a record of assaulting prostitutes; and James Sadler, a suspect in a later murder who was known to enjoy the company of prostitutes. It's worth noting that all three had solid alibis for the dates of the murders. Two of them weren't even in the country.'

'Plenty to be getting on with there, then,' Culverhouse said. 'Once we've got their family trees traced, we'll be able to see if there are any descendants living locally or working in professions of interest. We'll also need to draw up a list of potential persons of interest based on the suspects Debbie just gave. Modern day equivalents, if you like. Then I think it's time we had a word with a few of them.'

42

Suzanne Corrigan could feel her heart in her mouth as she held the envelope in front of her. She'd recognised the handwriting straight away. It was the same type of envelope as before — cream, half-A5, mottled and with the stamp perfectly aligned with the corners. Just seeing her name written in his handwriting was enough to send a chill down her spine.

Her first instinct was to put it down and go and tell her editor, but she knew she couldn't do that. The police had asked her not to. They needed to keep this under wraps for now, they said. At the same time, the envelope stuck to her hand like an industrial magnet, begging her to open it.

She knew she shouldn't. She knew she should take it straight to the police, but she also knew that if she did that she'd never know what was inside. After all, the letter was addressed to her. The contents were something the killer wanted *her* to see.

After a few seconds, her curiosity got the better of her and she slipped the end of her letter opener under the flap and gently tapped at the edge of the envelope. Once it was open, she poked the letter opener back in and used it to pull out the letter, taking care to check that there was nothing else in the envelope too. She was wary of leaving fingerprints, even though the police had told her the last letter didn't have any prints — other than hers — or anything they could use to identify the writer.

She opened the letter with her fingernail and held the bottom half down with the letter opener. That same handwriting. She'd been surprised that the police had scoffed when she suggested a handwriting profiler should look at the first letter. No longer seen as credible expert witness evidence, apparently.

She took a deep breath and began to read.

Dear Suzanne,

I can only presume you received my last letter. Forgive me for breaking with tradition but it seems those idiots need my help. So much for groundbreaking policing.

The third one was easy. They had no chance with that one. Too predictable in their movements. The fourth was a little spicier. That phone call made sure it was far less boring than otherwise. Gave me a bit of a run for my money. Shame I had to do it all myself though. Think they'd make an effort wouldn't you?

In case you haven't guessed by now I really like a chase. It's no fun when the police are clueless. Maybe you might ask them to consider a couple of things. It's amazing what you can do in plain sight. I thought my disguise was good but maybe I didn't need it after all.

I'll say no more. I'm sure you will hear from me again soon,

Suzanne. *Especially if the local police force continue to be as inept as they've already shown themselves to be.*

Jack

Patrick Sharp had only been given a very short amount of time to go through the letter, but in his mind that was all he needed.

'I'd say it's almost certainly from our man,' he said to Culverhouse. 'Yes, the style's very different but there's good reason for that. In the first letter he was emulating — almost copying — the original Dear Boss letter. In this one, he's writing as himself. Plus there's the fact that the handwriting's almost identical, not to mention the fact that he talks about the other two murders and the phone call — detail that wasn't released to the public.'

'So why the change of style?' Culverhouse asked.

'Could be many reasons, really, but the one I'd be cautious of is the possibility that he's had to change tack somehow. Things perhaps aren't going quite to plan for him, so he's having to change things from what he'd intended.'

'Diddums,' Culverhouse replied sarcastically.

'I wouldn't be quite so dismissive. If he's changing his plans, that could be disastrous for us. As things are, we know the date of his next murder plus we have an idea as to what sort of person his victim might be, as well as a shortlist of locations. It might sound vague, but it's more than most police forces have before a murder takes place. If he's being panicked somehow into changing his plan, we wouldn't have any of that. He could kill sooner, or later, and perhaps even a totally different victim.'

'Or not at all?'

'It's possible. I'd hope for your sake you're right.'

'Is it worth getting a handwriting analysis?' Wendy asked, jumping in.

Patrick Sharp chuckled. 'In a word, no. Especially not if you're talking about the kind of analysis where someone reckons they can tell a person's personality based on their handwriting. I'm afraid that's a load of old pony. You'd be better off seeing a medium.'

'It wouldn't be an option even if it wasn't a load of bollocks,' Culverhouse said. 'Our esteemed PCC wouldn't give us the budget anyway.'

'Even if it means the difference between catching our Ripper and not?' Wendy asked.

'Firstly, it doesn't. It means bugger all and would probably do more harm than good by leading us up the garden path. And secondly, you seem to be forgetting that we're expected to get world class results on a shoestring.'

Wendy had nothing to say in response to that. 'Aren't you a bit worried about the writer's breaking with tradition, though?' she asked Patrick Sharp.

'Not especially, no. Not in the sense that I'd doubt the veracity of the letter, anyway. It worries me that it might possibly signal a shift in his perception or MO, but that's purely speculation at the moment.'

'Do you think he might try stepping up his game?'

'It's possible. Above all, I'm pretty sure he'll stick to his MO. This has been far too carefully planned and orchestrated for him to throw that away right now. I'm fairly confident he'll stick to things like dates and times. He'll want to emulate the original Ripper killings. That's his whole *raison d'etre*. What he might do, though, is increase the stakes. He's already done it once by making that phone call in between the third and fourth murders, basically to tell you where he was. He's thriving on the chase and the increased tension.'

'So what, he wants to be caught?' Culverhouse asked.

'Not necessarily. He wants you to come close, certainly. I think the easiest way to describe it is that this is like a game to him. Imagine you're playing a computer game and you're winning easily and convincingly. For a bit more of a challenge, you might increase the difficulty level. Make it more fun. That's what our man is doing here.'

'You think there's a link with video games?'

'I doubt it. It's just the psychology behind it that's the same. We see it quite a lot in serial killers. They have an immense sense of power, but they like to and even need to have that power challenged occasionally, if only so they can win the battle and further validate their sense of power.'

'Oh, well I'm glad we could help him,' Culverhouse replied, folding his arms.

'As far as the content goes, I'd say he's sounding pretty confident. He's talking about the phone call making things far less boring. That all goes with his levelling-up the difficulty. A couple of things stand out. They're not for me to comment on, but I wonder if he's maybe thrown them in as little clues to up the ante even further. There's this mention of being in plain sight, plus the disguise which he says he maybe didn't need after all.'

'What, like a physical disguise?' Wendy asked.

'Who knows? That's not for me to say. There could be any number of meanings. The mention of being in plain sight is particularly intriguing, but at the same time could mean absolutely nothing. I mean, we already know that he's been walking around in plain sight inasmuch as he's been committing these crimes right under our noses. That might well be what he's referring to. The disguise is far more cryptic, perhaps, but worth looking into.'

Culverhouse stood and walked away from the table, shaking his head. 'No, I don't think so,' he said, rubbing his chin, the rough palm of his hand rasping against the stubble. 'I'm not convinced. How do we know he's not just trying to lead us down the wrong path? He's already done that before, trying to second guess us and use it to his advantage. What's to say he's not doing that again?'

Patrick Sharp just smiled. 'That, Jack, is what you're going to have to find out.'

By now, the team had had the opportunity to look further into the lives of the four dead women in order to try and find out if there were any links between them. They'd also been looking into doctors and surgeons living in Mildenheath as well as building a list of people who'd potentially be in a position to find out a lot about the women's lives.

They'd looked at the women's lives in as much detail as they could, but it seemed that there was little or no crossover. All except Emma Roche had Facebook profiles, and they'd cross-referenced the friends lists of the other three. They had only two mutual friends between them, which was quite remarkable considering the fact that they all lived in Mildenheath. One was a disabled woman living in a surrounding village who'd been housebound for three years and the other was a man who'd moved to New Zealand five years earlier for work.

'I had a look at the medical records,' Luke Baxter said, looking down to read off his notes. 'Keira Quinn had been taking medication for depression, as had Lindsay Stott. Marla

Collingwood had been going through CBT, a talking therapy, but had refused medication.'

'Isn't that quite high? Three out of four women being treated for depression?' Wendy asked.

'Depends how you look at it. Generally it'd be about one in four, but we're looking at women who live on their own, generally divorced or separated, not working. I'd be pretty bloody depressed too.'

Wendy decided not to bite. 'Who was the counsellor? Had Keira and Lindsay been having this CBT too?'

'Counsellor was a woman called Diana Kenning. She was on holiday when the last two women died, if that's what you're going to ask. And no, Keira and Lindsay had just been taking medication.'

'Did they have the same doctors?'

'Nope. Emma Roche and Keira Quinn were registered at the same surgery but saw different doctors. Lindsay Stott and Marla Collingwood were registered elsewhere.'

'Anyone else who'd have access to their medical histories?'

'Nothing requested by third parties,' Baxter replied curtly.

'I had a look through the list of doctors living in Mildenheath,' Frank Vine said. 'Mostly British or from the Indian subcontinent. No Polish or Eastern European, which I was looking out for based on what Debbie said about the Polish link in the original Ripper case. I did find something interesting, though. There's a doctor called Desmond Jordan living locally. Bit of an odd character by all accounts. Originally trained as a surgeon but took a diversion to become a GP. And guess what? He's American.'

'You thinking of a link with Tumblety, Frank?' Debbie asked, her voice betraying a frisson of excitement.

'It's possible. Tumblety was an American doctor living in Whitechapel and was heavily linked with the Ripper killings for quite a while.'

'Seems a bit tenuous to me,' Wendy said. 'Anything else to link them?'

'Not looked into it too far yet, but something did stand out. Tumblety was from Boston, right? Well, get this. Desmond Jordan is originally from Baltimore.'

Culverhouse stood and stared at Frank Vine for a few moments. 'Frank, I don't mean to be funny, but you are aware that they're about four hundred miles apart, aren't you?'

'Yeah, obviously, but they both begin with B! Got to be something in it, hasn't there?'

'Have we got anything better?' Culverhouse asked, exasperated.

'Not at the moment.'

'Great. Fucking great.'

'We're looking into the Polish community as a whole,' Steve Wing said. 'I'm in contact with the Polish church and community club down the road. Trying to see if there's anyone from Poland who trained as a doctor or surgeon before moving here. I'm also looking at the hairdresser route. Mainly because they're the sorts of people who hear all about people's lives. That and pub landlords, but we already know two of the women didn't go to pubs all that often and the other two went to different ones from each other, so I'm going to get onto phoning around all the local hairdressers to see if any of our four victims were on their client list.'

'Right. Good,' Culverhouse said. 'But why hasn't it been done already?'

'To be honest, guv, we've all been focusing mainly on the

medical side of things. Got to jump through hoops with the GMC, then cross-reference it all with census data and council tax records to see who lives locally. Then find their place of birth and run them through the PNC... It all takes time.'

'Well we don't have time,' Culverhouse said. 'That's running out fast, so let's get a move on, alright? The only name we've got so far is this Desmond Jordan. Probably best we get a statement and alibi from him for the nights of the murders. We don't want to spook him too much right now, so we'll visit a few other doctors as well. Word gets around and we don't want him to think he's our only suspect, particularly when we've got next to sod all to go on. Knight, could you go down and get a statement?'

'No problem. I'll do it later on today.'

'Right. And I want an update on everything by the end of the day. There's a lot of chasing and paperwork to do, so we need to get on top of it.'

Desmond Jordan's house was situated right on the edge of Mildenheath. Wendy noted that it would have been beyond the point at which the temporary roadblock would've been situated on the west side of the town. If the roadblocks had been put in place — presuming Jordan was the killer — could they have avoided the last two murders?

Wendy put these thoughts out of her head as she approached Desmond Jordan's house. The large crescent-moon driveway was damp with brown leaves, with green lichen coating the paved area on which the smart new Jaguar car was parked.

To the left of the house was a wide, white-doored garage and to the right were tall conifers, with a shingled driveway between them and the house. As Wendy got out of her car, she looked up this side driveway and noticed the familiar sight of Luke Baxter's car parked up the side of the house.

Just as she was comprehending what this meant, the large front door opened and DS Baxter stepped out, turning to shake the hand of a tall, professional looking man who she assumed to be Desmond Jordan. She couldn't hear what Baxter was saying, but Jordan's booming American lilt was unmistakeable.

'That's absolutely fine. I quite understand. If you need anything else, you know where to find me.'

With that, the door was closed and Wendy found herself facing Luke Baxter, who was looking partly very proud of himself and partly like a rabbit caught in the headlights.

'Luke, what are you doing here?'

'Interviewing Desmond Jordan. What does it look like?' he replied, walking past Wendy and heading to his car.

'That was my job! I was coming up here now to do that!'

'Well I've done it now, so you don't need to.'

Wendy got in between Baxter and his car, stopping him from opening the driver's side door.

'What's this all about, Luke? This isn't the first time you've got in the way and tried to make me look like some sort of incompetent idiot. Do you really think this is the sort of thing Culverhouse is impressed by? Because I can tell you now it isn't.' Deep down, Wendy wasn't even sure she believed her own words. 'Why couldn't you just leave it to me to speak to Jordan later on, like I said I would?'

'I was trying to save you time.'

'If that was the case, why didn't you ask me? Offer to help? Tell me you were doing it? But no, you went behind my back to make me look like a fucking idiot.'

'Wendy, you're taking this a bit far, don't you think? Desmond Jordan is—' He stopped and turned to look behind him, before continuing in a far quieter voice. 'Desmond Jordan is a person of interest. It's not the sort of thing we can afford to waste time on.'

'We've got over a month left before the next date, Luke. You know that. It could have waited another hour. There's procedure to be followed, you know? Certain ways things have to be done. You can't just ride roughshod over procedure because you think you can do things better.'

'What, like your darling Culverhouse?' Baxter replied, smirking.

'And what's that meant to mean?'

'Nothing, nothing at all,' he said, reaching for his door handle. Wendy batted his hand away.

'You just don't get it, do you? This is the police force, Luke. We are in charge of catching dangerous criminals. Possibly *the* most dangerous criminal in this particular case, and you're treating it as some sort of game. Some sort of power play. You need to grow up, and grow up fast.'

'Power play? Is that what you think it is?' Baxter laughed out loud. 'The only person who seems to have a problem with power is you. You've had a bug up your arse ever since I made DS. Listen, I'm sorry you've not had your efforts recognised but what can I say? Just keep trying, yeah?'

Wendy was too shocked to stop Luke from ushering her out of the way and getting into his car. She watched as he drove away, leaves and shingle kicked up by his tyres before she trundled over to her own car, got in and closed the door. She sat in silence for a few moments before turning the key in the ignition and driving away.

Desmond Jordan had been stewing ever since the police officer had visited a couple of days earlier. He wasn't used to having his integrity called into question. He'd always been a proud man; proud of his profession, proud of his work, proud of the way he conducted his life. He'd come a long way from humble beginnings, and he wasn't going to forget that.

Besides which, that fucking tart from over the road will have seen what was going on. He might well have come in an unmarked car and parked it up the side of the house, but that bitch never missed a trick. And hell, you could spot a copper a mile off around these parts, plain clothes or not. She was one of those women who needed to know everything that was going on. He knew she would've been straight on the phone to her crusty old friends from the WI within minutes. *You know that doctor who lives near me? The American one. Well it seems I was right all along. He's only got plain clothes detectives knocking on his door!*

It was purely routine, he'd said. They were trying to eliminate possible persons of interest, he said. But Desmond had seen enough police shows on the TV to know the routine.

They'd asked him for an alibi, for starters. How the hell was he meant to explain that? He'd had to settle for saying he'd been at home every night on his own. He'd just have to hope that the old bitch across the road didn't get a visit from PC Plod, else that might be blown out the water. She'd surely have seen him coming and going.

In his opinion, the Grouse and Partridge wasn't the best pub in town, but it was the closest, and right now he needed to get out of the house and have a drink. It was still the best part of a mile from his house on the edge of town, but the walk would probably do him good anyway.

Moving to the UK had been Bess's idea. She'd been fascinated by the country ever since she was a kid, and Desmond had to admit he was pretty happy to escape the US and start a new life over here, especially after what happened. It had been a less than conventional move, but then again his life had always been less than conventional.

He pulled himself up onto a stool at the bar and selected one of the six real ales on offer. He'd not been particularly keen on the British style of 'warm piss' beer, as he'd put it when he first came here, but he'd gradually got used to it and then came to actually quite like it.

His life was one huge tangle of knots. The lack of simplicity and normality rankled within him, giving him this almost interminable rage which kept bubbling under the surface, always threatening to break through, but which mercifully did so only rarely. He knew he wouldn't need much agitation today, though, and tried to keep himself to himself.

That was easier said than done. He'd barely been in the pub

twenty minutes, his first pint finished, after which he'd waited patiently to be served. A rough, loud woman who he'd heard talking from the other side of the pub had sidled up to the bar and shouted her order across at the young bar manager who was doing his best to keep up.

'Wait just a sec, love. I'll do yours next,' the barman replied, pacifying the woman.

'Actually, I think you'll find I was next,' Desmond said, his voice sure and certain. If there was one thing he hated, it was people pushing into a line or having some sort of warped sense of entitlement.

'Don't think so, mate. Never seen you in here before so you can wait your turn, yeah?' the woman replied, jabbing her finger in Desmond's direction. He could smell the fug of booze and fags wafting in his direction.

'So what if you've never seen me before? That gives you no right to push in. I waited my turn and it is my turn, so why don't you fuck off back under the rock you crawled out from?'

'You fucking what?' the woman yelled, not even noticing that the nervous young barman had already served her vodka and tonic and plonked it on the bar in front of her. 'Who the fuck do you think you are? In your posh suit and shoes. Think you're the fucking Big I Am, do you?'

'Don't try to make yourself look stupid, sweetheart. You manage it easily enough as it is,' Desmond replied, turning away from her.

'That's three-twenty, Lisa,' the barman said, trying to defuse the atmosphere in the only way he knew how.

'Get me another one,' the woman said to the barman as she picked up the glass and tossed its contents over the back of Desmond's head.

He had been trying so hard. So hard. Containing his rage had taken the ultimate effort from every fibre of his being, but that had pushed him over the edge. Without saying a word, he turned round, looked the woman in the eye and pummelled his fist into her eye socket.

Wendy had allowed herself a little smirk when she'd been called down to interview Desmond Jordan that evening. The arresting officers had seen that CID had him marked as a person of interest and were taking first dibs on interviews with him. Even more satisfying for Wendy was that she'd managed to get to him before Luke Baxter had.

Desmond Jordan's eyes looked dark and sullen as she and Culverhouse sat down opposite him at the desk and she took a few moments to look into his eyes.

'A respected family doctor walks into a local pub and punches a woman in the face, three days after being spoken to by the police about a spate of violent attacks on women. Not looking good, is it?' Wendy said, being uncharacteristically barbed. Her hatred for men who hit women was something she couldn't hide, no matter how much she tried.

Jordan had chosen not to have a solicitor present, presumably because he'd fallen under the common misapprehension that requesting a solicitor would somehow be an unspoken admission of guilt.

'Do you want to say anything about that?' Wendy asked.

'Yes, it was a stupid thing to do but I was provoked. I've been under a lot of stress recently, what with your colleague turning up at my house the other day.'

'Oh, so we'll just let you go and leave you alone, shall we? Wouldn't want you to be stressed, after all,' Culverhouse replied icily. 'I'm sure the families of the four murdered women won't mind.'

'I had nothing to do with that,' Jordan said, without a hint of emotion in his voice.

'I never said you did. But I don't think the families would be happy if we didn't do our job and investigate properly, which, as you were told by DS Baxter, involves speaking to a large list of people of certain professions. I know that if I were in your shoes, I'd want the killer caught.'

Desmond Jordan said nothing.

'This isn't going to do your career much good, is it?' Wendy said. 'Conviction for violent assault on a woman? I'm pretty sure that would result in being struck off.'

'Not necessarily, no. I'd have to go before a GMC panel who'd decide if I was fit to practise. *If* I was convicted, that is. As you well know, you've only arrested me. The police don't convict; the courts do.'

Wendy smiled. 'And you think we're going to have any trouble getting a conviction? After you punched a woman in the middle of a pub full of people?'

'I'd like to ask you a little more about your whereabouts in the early hours of the thirty-first of August, seventh of September and twenty-ninth of September,' Culverhouse said. 'You told Detective Sergeant Baxter that you were at home on your own on those nights.'

'Yes, I stay at home on my own every night. When I get home from work, I like to wind down at home.'

'And your wife and kids are away for a while, is that right?'

'Yes, they've gone back to Baltimore for eight weeks. To visit family.'

'That's a long time to be away, isn't it? Was that your idea?' Wendy asked, firing her questions at Jordan.

'I don't know who first suggested it. We both go back occasionally, but Bess can get more time away, obviously. As they're staying with family it's only really the flights that cost money. It costs them next to nothing while they're out there, so they make the most of it.'

'Your wife works as your practice manager, doesn't she? How can she have that much time away? And what about your kids?'

'They're homeschooled. And we get a temp in while Bess is away. As much as I love my wife, it's not a particularly difficult job. We use an agency who supply experienced people. It's not a problem.'

Culverhouse shuffled in his seat. 'Must be nice for them to be out of your hair for a few weeks. Gives you free reign to be the man you want to be.'

'I can see you've been married, Inspector,' Jordan said, smiling. 'It has its advantages, but mostly I just get on with my work.'

'And your nice relaxing evenings,' Wendy added. 'During which you never leave the house, is that right?'

'On the whole, yes. I mean, I might occasionally pop out to the shop or something but generally speaking, yes.'

'Which is interesting, because one of your neighbours said she sees you leave the house quite a bit in the evenings. She couldn't give us any specific dates, but she reckoned it must easily be more than half of the nights.' As Wendy spoke, she could see Jordan's jaw clenching, his nostrils flaring. 'Is that when you pop to the shop? Because I don't know about you, but personally I'd get all the stuff in one go. Quite a pain to have to go out on more than half of your evenings.'

'If you're talking about the woman I presume you're talking about, you'll know that she's nuts,' Jordan said quietly. 'Quite frankly, she's a sensationalist.'

Culverhouse changed tack quickly, trying to throw Jordan off balance. He removed four photographs from the brown folder in front of him and placed them in front of Jordan. 'Keira Quinn, Lindsay Stott, Emma Roche and Marla Collingwood. Do you recognise any of them?'

'No, should I?' Jordan replied.

'I should imagine so. We know they weren't patients of yours, but at least two of these photos have been on the news and in the papers recently,' Wendy said.

'I don't watch the news or read the papers. Most of it's horse shit.'

'That's one thing we can agree on,' Culverhouse said, removing a further five photographs from the folder. This time, they were close-up photos of the victims taken at the crime scene. 'Perhaps this might help. This is how they were found, after they'd been killed.'

Desmond Jordan spent a few seconds looking at each of the photographs before he looked up at Culverhouse.

'I must say, you don't seem too surprised or disgusted. Most people have some sort of visible reaction when they see a murder victim,' Wendy said.

'I'm a doctor. These pictures are no more shocking to me than a pair of handcuffs is to you.'

'I think I'd still expect some sort of reaction,' Wendy replied, narrowing her eyebrows.

'Blessed is he who expects nothing, for he shall never be disappointed. Alexander Pope.'

'You're clearly a very wise man,' Culverhouse said, exchanging a look with Wendy. 'So perhaps you could start by telling us where you really were on those three nights.'

48

On the inside, Desmond Jordan was reeling. Externally, though, he had to keep a calm head and try not to let things spiral out of control. He knew that bitch across the road would be the one to fuck everything up for him. And now there was nothing he could do about it.

Fortunately, she didn't know the reason why he'd been going out most nights and he'd pleaded with the police to make sure she didn't find out. In exchange, he'd had to tell them absolutely everything.

He'd had to tell them that he'd been sleeping with the temp while his wife and kids were visiting family in Baltimore. He'd had to tell them that he'd go round to her place three or four nights a week, knowing that ears would prick up and tongues would wag if she ever came over to his. If word ever got back to the woman over the road, he knew damn well that Bess would find out and that'd be his marriage over. His wife was a pretty forgiving woman, but even she had her limits.

It was never something that he'd intended to happen. But then that's what they all said, wasn't it? *It just kind of happened.*

Yes, it had probably been his idea for Bess and the kids to take a break, but it wasn't as though he was just shipping them off to get them out of the way. Jack and Lyra had done particularly well in their last assessments, so he figured they could do with a break.

Homeschooling the kids hadn't been as straightforward as Bess had made it sound. She'd been homeschooled herself back in the US, but found it difficult to cope with doing it herself in the UK. As a result, they'd hired an au pair with experience in homeschooling who'd teach the kids while Desmond and Bess were out at work. As far as Desmond was concerned, this completely defeated the object as the idea was that by being homeschooled the kids would see far more of their parents. In his opinion, they could've just been sent to the local school and he could've saved a packet on what he was paying the au pair. But no, Bess was insistent. Her first few years of school in the US had been hell for her, with the bullying getting so bad that her parents had pulled her out and homeschooled her. She didn't want the same for her kids, she said.

Bess wasn't the sort of woman who always got what she wanted, but if she felt particularly strongly about something she was like a dog with a bone. That was one of the things which had first attracted him to her. That strong temperament and independent will was something he really admired, but some-times even he needed a break.

He'd done his best to minimise his worries in life. Having a plan always helped, he found. He'd always been clear and methodical in his ways — that was one of the things that got him through med school — but he really hadn't planned for the whole sleeping-with-the-temp thing. Fortunately for him, that had been his biggest and only real worry in life up until now. He could be quite a highly strung person when under stress, which was why he stuck rigorously to his life plan.

Within five years the mortgage would be paid off. Then he'd look to sell the practice and he and Bess could both retire. The kids would be ready to go into the world of work — or, more likely, university — and he and his wife would be free to do whatever they wanted. If Bess got her way, it'd probably involve a move back to the US, but Desmond wasn't keen. Fortunately for him, it wasn't something she brought up often so there was a chance he might be able to avoid a showdown over it.

He'd been bailed over the incident in the pub, 'pending further enquiries'. He wasn't sure what other enquiries they could possibly make, and he hoped that they were trying to avoid having to charge him. He'd inform the General Medical Council of his arrest anyway. He knew from speaking to other doctors who'd had incidents in the past that the GMC's biggest bugbear was when members didn't tell them something had happened. If he told them, there was a decent chance he might be able to continue practising. If he didn't tell them and they found out another way — which they always did — he would have no chance.

Could he deal with that? Financially, probably. He could sell the practice and pay off his mortgage. The money he'd have left over would probably allow him to make do. If not, he could take a part-time job somewhere to make ends meet. That wasn't his main worry. It would be the indignity of it all. He'd worked so hard to get where he was, despite his difficult beginnings, and he wasn't about to let a lifetime's hard work go to waste.

49

Helen took a large gulp of her chilled white wine and finally put pen to paper. She'd rehearsed almost every word, over and over in her head ever since she'd left Jack. Left him again.

No, she mustn't think that. She didn't leave him; he forced her away. Forced her again.

She knew she needed to keep a level head. She'd learnt plenty of coping strategies, which were fine for the usual daily stresses and trivialities of life, but how was anybody in their right mind meant to cope with this, let alone their wrong mind?

She couldn't risk letting her feelings run away with her, but this letter needed writing. She had to tell him what was what. Calm, unemotional, matter of fact.

Dear Jack,

I'm writing to tell you that I've left the country again. I thought things might have changed, but evidently they haven't.

I'm sorry things didn't work out and that we couldn't find our peace. I tried. I really did. But we're obviously two different people. We're poisonous together. When I left the last time I eventually managed to find my peace. I found myself. I discovered all that was wrong and I managed to find a way through it. I realised who I really was.

I thought I could use that to come back and patch things up, but coming back just opened up old wounds and reminded me of the person I used to be — the life I want to forget.

You'll note this letter is postmarked from Paris. Don't read anything into that. Call it a brief stopover. I won't be getting in touch again any time soon, but I will pass your message on to Emily. I promise. She deserves to know the truth, no matter how unpalatable it is. And as you rightly say, she has a right to see you — if she wants to. She certainly hasn't been keen up to now.

I hope all is well with work and life and that you can find your own peace in time.

Helen.

The information the team had amassed by now was extraordinary. They'd been tasked with uncovering every detail about each of the four women's lives, as well as building up profiles of every doctor and surgeon in Mildenheath. They'd built up a database of Polish people of interest and started to look at links between the lives of the women, including their medical histories, social lives and any local pub or businesses they frequented.

Mildenheath being a town of barely 35,000 people, there were, of course, a fair few crossovers. What really stood out, though, was a piece of information uncovered by DC Debbie Weston, who'd spent the last couple of days phoning every hairdresser in the town, amongst other things. Mildenheath had a fair few hairdressers' shops, but that was nothing compared to the number of mobile hairdressers listed in the Yellow Pages. It hadn't taken her long before she'd got a hit.

'I spoke to Terri Kinsella, the owner of Terri's, a shop on Eastfield Road,' Debbie said. 'I didn't believe it at first, but apparently all four women went there to get their hair cut.'

'Blimey,' Culverhouse replied, finally having found something to jolt his mind away from thinking of the letter he'd received from Helen. He had been expecting something of the kind, but it still rankled. He knew, though, that he had bigger fish to fry. As much as he desperately wanted to see Emily again, he'd waited years already and a few more days or weeks wouldn't hurt. He felt guilty for putting the job first again, but reconciled that with the assertion that he was trying to save someone's life.

'When did they all last have an appointment?' he asked, getting his mind back on the task in hand.

'That's the weird thing. Marla Collingwood used to go about once every three weeks. She was quite fussy about her hair, apparently. But then Emma Roche and Keira Quinn only went every now and again. Lindsay Stott was a bit more regular with her appointments, but even she hadn't been in for a while. It's a very popular shop, though. It's huge, and their prices are really good.'

'Great, I'll remember that next time I need a short back and sides,' Culverhouse said. 'So this whole idea of the silent confidant might not be so strange after all.'

'Exactly. And get this. I asked the owner if the women went to see a particular hairdresser. They all went to see the same person.'

The officers in the incident room were deadly silent, waiting for Debbie to provide them with the name of their new prime suspect.

'Fucking spit it out, will you?' Culverhouse barked.

'It was Queenie Kinsella. Her mother.'

'F... What?' the DCI replied.

'I know. She's eighty-three, apparently, but people specifically request her to do it because she's so good. People see her like a mother figure.'

'Well, she is. She's Terri's mother, for a start,' Frank Vine proffered helpfully.

Culverhouse stood with his hands on his hips. 'Are we all missing the fucking point here? The woman's eighty-three! How do you think she managed to kill four fit young women? Not to mention putting on a man's voice in the phone box that night. I mean, I'm sure she's a brilliant hairdresser but she's not a fucking shapeshifter.'

'Yeah, it is a bit weird, I know, but it's the only lead we've got. You have to admit, with everything else being totally unconnected, it's odd that they all went to the same hairdresser, isn't it?'

'Yes, Debbie, it's odd,' Culverhouse said. 'But so are BDSM, sadomasochism and morris dancing. Just because it's odd doesn't make it suspicious. Apart from morris dancing, that is.'

'I can get down there and speak to her if you like, guv,' Wendy asked. 'I can't go for an hour or two, but I don't think they'd be open yet anyway, would they?'

'I've got her home address,' Debbie said. 'I didn't think it would be a good idea to be sending police round to the shop. Apparently she only works mornings, so she'll be home by one-thirty.'

'Okay, I'll pop over at some point this afternoon,' Wendy replied.

'Want me to go, guv?' Luke Baxter said, jumping in. 'I can probably pop over and meet her after she finishes at the shop. Get on top of things as quickly as possible. No time to lose and all that,' he added, looking pointedly at Wendy.

'I'm quite capable of doing it myself, thanks, Luke.'

'Actually,' Culverhouse said, diffusing the growing atmosphere, 'why don't you both go along? It might do you good to work together for once instead of constantly trying to wind each other up.'

Wendy looked at Luke and tightened her jaw. This wasn't going to be her idea of fun.

51

It took a solid thirty seconds of Wendy standing with her finger pressed on the doorbell for Queenie Kinsella to hear it. Once the noise of the vacuum cleaner had finally wound down and she'd trotted over to the door and opened it, Wendy was already wishing she could leave.

'Queenie Kinsella? I'm Detective Sergeant Wendy Knight and this is—'

'Detective Sergeant Luke Baxter,' he added, interrupting.

'Ah yes, Terri spoke to your friend on the phone earlier. Do come in, won't you? I'm sorry if I didn't hear the bell at first,' she said, continuing to talk as she waddled through into the kitchen. 'It's this blasted hoover. Can't hear a thing over it. Always having to run it round, too. Gets harder and harder to keep a house clean as you get older, see. I thought it'd be easier after my Alf went, but if anything the blasted place has got dirtier. He was always tracking muck through the house, leaving pistons and spark plugs and god knows what in the sink. Mucky bugger, he was.'

'Must be very difficult,' Wendy offered.

'Oh, it's alright. Wouldn't have it any other way, I suppose. I've got my friends and family and I've still got my work. Rare to be able to do what I do at my age, but I've always loved it. I love the gossip and the chat, and meeting people. I think that's what keeps you going. Want a cup of tea?'

'Please,' Wendy replied.

Luke, for once, agreed.

'Not much left in the way of family, mind. There's only Terri, who you know, and my son, Paul. He owns the shop next door to Terri's. They pop in whenever they can, but they're so busy with their work. You know what it's like, being young people yourself. I suppose that's why I still work at Terri's place, in a way. Get to spend time with the both of them. Or at least be in the same place as them, anyway.'

'Your work, Mrs Kinsella. You work mornings, is that right?' Wendy asked, trying to steer the conversation.

'That's right, love, yes. I usually get there about ten o'clock. The shop opens at nine, but get there a bit later as I like to watch my morning telly. Plus I can only really do about three or so hours a day, so if I get there at nine I'd have to be gone by twelve and a lot of my customers can only make it on their lunch breaks, see. Busy old world.'

Even though Wendy was doing her best to direct the conversation, Luke Baxter's backside had barely touched the kitchen chair before he'd jumped in and tried to take control.

'Do you know your clients well?' he asked.

'Some of them, yes. We have a good old natter most of the time. I think a lot of them feel like they can talk to me, you know. An older person. The voice of experience, maybe,' Queenie said, breaking off into a laugh which sounded more like a cackle.

I'm surprised they can get a word in edgeways, Wendy thought. Before she could say anything, Baxter had jumped in again.

'Are these women customers of yours?' he said, taking four photographs out of his inside jacket pocket and putting them down on the table, forcing Queenie to put down the sugar jar and trot over to take a look.

'Ooh, yes. All of them. Nice girls. Troubled, but then isn't everybody?'

'Do you know their names?' Wendy asked, getting in before Luke.

'I know everyone's name, love,' Queenie replied. 'You don't do a job like mine in a town like this without knowing everyone. That drunk looking one is Lindsay. Lindsay Scott, I think. No, Stott. Yes, with a T. The one there is Keira Quinn. Nice Irish name. Always remember that. She doesn't come in that often, though. Same with this one. Another Irish name, I think. Roche. Emma Roche.' She chuckled as she picked up the final photograph. 'Ah, yes. Marla Collingwood. She practically lives in the shop. One of our more regular customers. Lovely lady.'

'Mrs Kinsella, I'm afraid Keira Quinn and Lindsay Stott died a few weeks back,' Wendy said.

'Oh, I know that, love. I might be old, but I'm not senile. I seen the papers like everyone else.'

'You just don't seem too shocked, that's all.'

'What, after a month and a half? Sweetie, I'm eighty-four next month. I've seen my fair share of death. Takes a lot to faze me.'

'Did you not find it a bit odd that two of your customers died within a few days of each other?' Wendy asked.

'Not especially, no. It happens. We have hundreds of

customers. Probably more. Want a drop of brandy in your tea, love?' she said, gesturing to Luke.

'No thanks. I must ask you to keep this confidential for now, but Emma Roche and Marla Collingwood also died recently.'

Wendy shot Luke an icy glare. This had not been discussed or authorised. Knowing Queenie Kinsella's loose tongue, it was highly unlikely that what he'd just told her was going to stay within these four walls.

'Oh. Well that is a terrible shame. And all so young. Tell me, were the other two murdered as well?'

Wendy tried to hold Luke's eye contact as if to say *Don't commit to anything*.

'I'm afraid so,' Luke replied.

'Oh. Well your lot are going to be busy, then, aren't you?' Queenie replied. 'By my reckoning, that makes it a serial killer. I seen some programmes on it.'

'It does, yes,' Luke said.

'We're not certain the deaths are connected yet,' Wendy interjected. 'We're still investigating. But we're looking for links. And as you know, all four women were customers of yours so we needed to speak to you to find out more about them and what might link them.'

'Well, I don't know, love,' the old woman replied, sitting down and stirring her tea. 'I mean, they were all nice girls. Troubled. Maybe something caught up with them.'

'How do you mean?' Wendy asked.

'Well they all liked a drink, for starters. But who doesn't?' She cackled again. 'They weren't your typical office workers, if you see what I mean.'

'I'm afraid we don't,' Baxter replied, pressing Queenie for more detail.

'Let's just say that I know at least two of them used to work as ladies of the night, so to speak. Not your usual grotty kind. Private work, I mean. That Marla used to drink a lot. Sometimes she would've been in the pub all morning before coming in. I don't know where she got her money. She'd spend a fair packet in our shop, to be fair. I think she tried to paper over the cracks, if you see what I mean. And that Emma'd had trouble. Apparently her husband had been a bit of a wrong'un. They'd broken up and he'd buggered off back to Ireland, thank God.'

'You seem to know a lot about them,' Wendy said.

'Oh yes. You get to hear about all sorts of people's problems in my job. I think that's why a lot of people get their hair cut so often. It's not the hairdo they want, it's the shoulder to lean on. You get some right sorts come through our shop. All sorts of life stories. It'd amaze you, it really would. One woman, right, called Amanda, she comes in probably about once a month or so. Lives down on the Hampton Road. Now she used to be a bloke called Derek. Get that! None so queer as folk.'

It struck Wendy that Queenie's loose tongue might perhaps have done more damage than she realised.

52

'What the fuck, Luke? Seriously, what the fuck?' Wendy yelled as she slammed the car door and glared at her colleague.

'I beg your pardon?' Baxter replied, starting the ignition on the car.

'What the hell did you think you were doing? Telling her that Emma Roche and Marla Collingwood were dead? That's not public knowledge! We were told to keep that under wraps!'

'No, we were told not to leak it to the press. Queenie Kinsella is a potential witness, if not a suspect, so we needed to tell her so that we could see how she reacted.'

'Are you sure the DCI's going to see it that way?' Wendy asked, turning her head to stare out through the raindrops which were skidding down the window.

'I don't see why not. He quite often tends to see things from my point of view.'

'Tell me about it.'

'Ah-ha. Is that your problem? The fact that the guv actually likes me and respects the way I do things? You had a bug up your arse ever since he told you to come and speak to the old woman with me. You wanted to go on your own, and when you found out you were going with me you weren't interested.'

'Shut up, Luke. You know that's not the case. I just know what you're like. You don't play by the rules. You're incapable of it. That's why Culverhouse likes you. Not because you're a good police officer, but because you're a younger version of him. And he's a fucking dinosaur of a bygone age as it is.'

'I'll let him know that,' Baxter replied. 'I'm sure he'll be delighted.'

'It's nothing I've not told him before. What if Queenie Kinsella now goes blabbing around the salon about the fact that two more women have died and we're looking for a serial killer? What good do you think that's going to do?'

Baxter snorted. 'Probably a lot more good than has been done so far, sitting around doing nothing. At the very least it'll flush him out. Bring him above the surface of the water.'

'Either that or we'll end up with mobs of vigilantes on the streets.'

'You say that like it's a bad thing. If you ask me, we could do with all the help we can get right now.'

'Are you kidding me? Luke, *we* don't even know who the killer is. What's to say a group of mob-handed louts are going to get the right person? Any poor bugger walking along the street on his own is going to get picked on and put in huge danger.'

'Unlikely. Do you want results or not?'

Wendy had nothing else to say to him. She shook her head in disgust and went back to watching raindrops chase each other down the window.

53
23RD OCTOBER

Helen's heels clip-clopped across the polished surface of the airport terminal's floor, her small case trundling along behind her, the wheels skipping over every chip in the tiles. She passed shop after shop: fashion accessories, books, electronics. It had always struck her as bizarre how airports were like small town centres with no permanent residents. Everyone was just passing through. A nice metaphor for life, she thought.

She thumbed the passport in her jacket pocket, thankful — not for the first time — that she'd managed to secure her new identity before passport and identity restrictions in her new home country had been tightened. She was sure it wouldn't be foolproof; Jack would find a way if he wanted to. The fact that it was a genuine passport meant there'd be a paper trail, but she'd made sure there was no link between her old identity and her new one.

She'd kept her forename — that was important to her. Getting used to an entirely new name would've been too risky, especially if she'd not responded to it or — worse — had spun round whenever someone said the word 'Helen'.

She backtracked slightly and wandered into the bookshop, stopping to look at that week's top ten fiction bestsellers. It was the usual depressing mix of chick-lit and fantasy, with the odd promising title thrown in. She picked up one called *The Stones of Petreus*, a novel about a man who fakes his own death and ends up roaming the world, becoming embroiled in a criminal conspiracy. It wasn't her usual style of book, but looked well-written, so she took it to the counter and bought it, before heading back into the main departures lounge and sitting on a cold metal bench.

People-watching had always been a hobby of hers. She liked to try and guess who people were, what they did for a living, where they were going. The holidaymakers were always pretty clear: the t-shirts, shorts and sandals in October gave it away. So too were the business passengers, suited and booted with laptops out, or mumbling into their mobile phones. But it was the others who interested her. The people who were flying out for funerals, to visit sick relatives, to research books, to build a school in Ghana. She was one of those too, she supposed. This was certainly no holiday for her.

She looked up at the departures board and scanned down to find her flight number. It was still showing nothing, but the flight four slots before hers had started to board, so it wouldn't be long. She shuffled to get comfortable and opened the first page of the book.

54

31ST OCTOBER

Jack Culverhouse sidled into Chief Constable Hawes's office knowing damn well what the topic of conversation was going to be. The pressure had been growing for weeks, months, and he could sense that things were about to come to a head.

'I'm in a very tricky situation, Jack,' the Chief Constable said as he handed a glass of water across the desk to Culverhouse. 'You and I both know your style is... unconventional. But it's always got results. And while the operational decisions of the force have been down to me, that's been fine. But I'm being leant on from above.'

'So what you're saying is the PCC doesn't like me?' Culverhouse asked, knowing the answer to the question before he'd even asked it.

Hawes chuckled and looked down into his glass. 'The PCC doesn't like anybody. You know how much this job has become focused around targets and numbers in recent years. Well that's nothing compared to the PCC's job. That's all about numbers and targets. He has nothing else. And as far as he's concerned, he's authorised a huge amount of spending on this investigation and he's got nothing except four dead bodies. And I don't think I need to go into the whole thing about being the most underfunded—'

'No, you don't,' Culverhouse interrupted. 'What does he actually think goes through our minds exactly? That we're just sat around eating doughnuts and not really caring if we catch the guy at all? That it really doesn't matter to us, as long as he provides the budget?'

Hawes steepled his hands and leant back in his chair. 'I really don't know what he thinks. That's the problem. All I know is that he's seriously pushing for this "streamlining" initiative as he calls it. Bringing all of CID under one roof.'

'Tell me one thing, sir. Why won't he come down here and do this himself? Why's he using you as his messenger? We never see hide nor hair of him. If you ask me, it sounds pretty cowardly.'

The Chief Constable raised his hands in mock surrender. 'Don't ask me. I'm not exactly happy about it either.'

'So he can't even have the balls to come down here and tell me he's shuffling me into a backroom to suck Malcolm Pope's cock?'

Hawes raised an eyebrow. 'I'm not entirely sure that's on his list, but you never know. The PCC has his favourites, Jack. You and I aren't two of them. And we're certainly not doing ourselves any favours on this investigation. Between you and me, if we don't get results — fast — then I don't think you can count on being made SIO on any major cases in the future.'

For once, Culverhouse was speechless. As the most senior and experienced CID detective at Mildenheath, he'd been used to being the Senior Investigating Officer on any major cases in and around the town. He knew he was a big fish in a small pond and that the only reason he held the position he did was because of that. In a larger CID unit, he'd be shipped off as part of the old guard in no time at all. Modern policing didn't treat men like Jack Culverhouse well, and it was his saving grace that Mildenheath was far from being at the forefront of modern policing.

Their unconventional setup and style hadn't come at the expense of results, though. Mildenheath always got results and Jack Culverhouse always got results. That had kept Hawes happy. But since the PCC had come in, things were different. He'd been looking for a reason to replace Culverhouse and Hawes ever since day one, and this would provide him with the perfect opportunity.

'And what happens to you if this all goes ahead?' he asked the Chief Constable.

'Who knows? Early retirement, probably. You don't just preside as Chief Constable over a failed serial killer investigation and get away with it. It wouldn't be my choice, either, really. The PCC can call on me to resign if he feels it's in the best interests of the police force. And, let's face it, I'd only need to put the wrong type of milk in his tea to fill that criteria.'

'And me? I'll be filing paperwork in an office somewhere, I presume.'

'I doubt that, Jack. You wouldn't stand for that. In most cases, he'd probably do that because that'd be his only option. So many officers these days are mercenaries who'd take that as a punishment of sorts. If the CID departments are merged, though, we'd have too many DCIs. At least one would have to be made redundant. Cost-cutting, they'd call it. And he knows that'd be the ultimate humiliation for you. Plenty would take the money and run, but he knows you don't give a toss about money.'

'I don't give a toss about lots of things,' Culverhouse replied. 'But my job's not one of them.'

The Chief Constable leant forward and nodded his head slowly. 'Then you know what you have to do, Jack.'

It had all gone quiet on the Western Front. He wasn't surprised; he didn't have much faith in the police these days.

The Victorian police had an excuse: they were living and working in a time in which recent advances in forensic science and criminal profiling hadn't been made. They had that against them. The police of today didn't have that excuse. They had all the tools at their disposal, all the evidence and clues they needed and they still weren't capable.

He wasn't upset. He was quite pleased, actually. He'd predicted this might be the case. As a citizen, of course, he was dismayed, but that didn't matter too much. He wouldn't be a citizen for long.

He'd read all of the newspapers that day as a matter of course, like he did every day. He'd browsed through all of the major online news sources, too. Things had gone quiet. It was a sad situation when even a modern day version of the most famous and ruthless serial killer of all time was loose on the streets and it was still being knocked off the front pages by the latest celebrity relationship break-ups and shock-horror news stories about immigration.

He had very little faith in anyone or anything these days. That had all gone long ago. When everyone else had finished caring about the important stuff, he'd decided to join them.

He wasn't panicked or anxious, but his sense of awareness had been heightened dramatically. He was now acutely aware of the passing of time. He knew exactly what time of day it was at any given moment, and he certainly knew what the date was.

He was counting down.

Stress levels had been building steadily at Mildenheath CID. By now, the whole team was aware of what was at stake. Up until now they'd been able to operate more or less as an autonomous CID department with the Chief Constable leaving them to their own devices as long as they got results. Now, though, they had less than forty-eight hours before they knew the Ripper would strike again and they'd be faced with closure, mergers and redundancies.

For Wendy, it was all about little pleasures. She'd had enough stress to deal with in recent months and years, what with her first serial murder case resulting in the killer being found a little too close to home, her partner being murdered and then the trauma of the miscarriage she'd suffered. Work had been a saving grace for her, allowing her to throw herself into something and have something into which to channel her energy.

She knew that she'd probably personally be safe should Mildenheath CID be merged into county HQ, but that wasn't the point. She had friends and colleagues who wouldn't be quite so safe, plus she had a certain affinity for this place. It was where her dad had worked all those years before. It was where she'd worked, where she'd built her career. It was her home. She didn't want to move to some faceless glass building any more than the others did.

One such little pleasure was being able to at least look forward to her lunchtime snack each day. A new deli-cum-café had opened around the corner from the station, offering something a little bit different from the usual Mildenheath fare. Their gourmet sandwiches were to die for; huge slabs of granary bread filled to bursting with your choice of filling. She'd been slowly working her way through the menu and had even been tempted towards some of the more chic foods, including a chickpea and quinoa salad a couple of days before which had been surprisingly alright. Today, it was the turn of the tuna melt.

Or at least it would have been, if she hadn't opened the fridge in the kitchen and found that it had gone missing. She'd heard stories from friends up at Milton House about things going missing from fridges (another reason to oppose the merger), but to date there'd been nothing of the sort at Mildenheath. The joys of working with a small team meant that everyone knew — and respected — everyone. Well, nearly everyone.

Just as she was racking her brains trying to remember if she'd actually put it in there or not, in walked Luke Baxter, complete with one tuna melt hanging out of his mouth.

'Alright, Wend?' he said as he swallowed another mouthful. 'Fancy a cuppa?'

It wasn't the fact that he'd stolen her lunch that upset her most. It was the fact that he'd shortened her name. Only one person had ever been allowed to do that, and that was her brother, Michael.

'Is that my lunch you're eating?' she asked as calmly as she could.

'Well, no, it's my lunch technically,' he replied, flicking the switch on the kettle.

'Where did you get it from?'

'The fridge. Didn't have a name on it. Presumed it was up for grabs.'

'Since when has anything in that fridge been "up for grabs"?' she shrieked, her voice raising a good two octaves.

'Er, since we all contribute to it?' he replied, almost as a question. 'The milk, chocolates, orange juice...'

'But not my bloody lunch!' Wendy yelled, snatching the tuna melt from his hand and throwing it in the bin. 'You're doing this on purpose, aren't you?' she said, putting her face so close to his that she could smell the tuna and mayonnaise. 'You're just doing this to be a dickhead.'

'Oh get over yourself, Wend.'

'Do *not* call me that!'

'Jesus, who put sandpaper in your knickers? Chill out. You won't last five minutes at Milton House with an attitude like that.' He turned to walk off.

'And what would you know?' she yelled, grabbing his arm. 'You don't have a clue how to treat people. You just walk all over them, trying to get what you want. That's not how things are done here. That's not how you earn respect.'

'Well it certainly worked in earning me my Sergeant's stripes, didn't it? I seem to recall it taking you a lot longer than that.'

'Yeah, because I didn't act like an arse-licking little shit to my superior officers!' By now, Wendy's voice had risen to a level which had attracted the attention of the other officers in the adjoining incident room.

'I think you need to take some time away, Wend. Maybe get to grips with your anger issues. It's clearly causing you a problem,' Baxter said, smirking like a Cheshire cat.

'How fucking dare you—' Wendy was cut off mid-flow by the imposing figure of DCI Culverhouse wading into the room, his voice flattening the atmosphere immediately.

'Enough! What's this all about?'

DS Baxter laughed. 'I picked up her sandwich by mistake and she flipped out. I think she needs some time away, guv.'

'What the fuck?' Wendy was incredulous. 'He *stole* my lunch on purpose and then deliberately tried winding me up about it! I've had enough of his attitude and the way he treats people.'

'Stop!' Culverhouse barked. 'In case you two fucking numpties hadn't realised, we've got a pretty bloody big case on our hands. The last thing we need is two of our officers at each other's throats. What good do you think that's going to do?'

Luke and Wendy looked at each other, not saying a word.

'Now, I want the two of you to go home. I can't risk you fucking this investigation up at the last minute. You've both completed your actions, right?'

'Yes,' Wendy replied, quietly. 'Just awaiting further instructions and preparing for tomorrow night, guv.'

'Good,' Culverhouse replied. 'In that case, you can both consider your work on the case to be completed.'

'What? But it's not finished yet!' Baxter pleaded.

'I'm not kicking you off. I'm telling you I don't have anything more for you to do. Tomorrow night will be a response situation for CID. It's down to the officers on the ground to take over. We can manage without you both until the morning after. You can spend tomorrow evening, after you've both calmed down, meeting up in a pub somewhere and talking through your differences. Because if I'm going to hold this unit together, I bloody well need you both to cooperate.'

'A pub?' Wendy said, almost laughing. 'Tomorrow night? With respect, guv, I'd rather be here working on the biggest case we've ever had rather than in a pub. And anyway, if the town's being shut off we won't be able to get near a pub.'

'There are villages. You'll manage. Now do as you're told and fuck off.'

57

The lot of a journalist — aside from the long hours and terrible pay — was the balance between loyalty to her sources and loyalty to her job.

Suzanne Corrigan had been updated by DS Wendy Knight about the investigation, but on the strict proviso that none of it was to even be hinted at in the newspapers.

Wendy had told Suzanne some incomplete details in order to test the water. She trusted Suzanne as a source of information following receipt of the Dear Boss letter. Of course, they'd had to probe her whereabouts on the nights of the murders and investigate her background in order to work out why she of all people had received the letter. Put simply, Suzanne Corrigan was not a person under suspicion, and Wendy now wanted to use this opening to foster more positive relations with at least one member of the local press.

It was all about give and take. Suzanne had provided them with a vital piece of evidence and Wendy would keep her in the loop as to what was going on. As soon as something was publishable, Suzanne would have the scoop. In the meantime, she'd had to report only the bare bones, with the police careful not to release any details which would have allowed anyone to draw the obvious links between the killings. The fact that the same person could be responsible for more than one — or all — of them was pretty much accepted as public knowledge, and it had hit the sweet spot between raising awareness and limiting hysteria.

For Suzanne, the decision was gut-wrenching. She knew that this story would easily be the biggest local news story of the year, if not the decade, and would also make for huge national news. She thought back to the press scramble over the Yorkshire Ripper, Harold Shipman and the Ipswich murders and realised that she had an enormous opportunity to break one of the biggest crime stories of all time. A madman terrorising a small English town by recreating the murders of Jack the Ripper? It was pure gold.

Running with the story would, without doubt, completely destroy her relationship with the police. She might get a big payday from the paper, who'd make a mint by selling the story up to the nationals, but it would almost certainly be the last crime story she worked on locally.

All her journalistic instincts told her to go for it, but there was something stopping her. She knew from previous stories on the paper what Wendy Knight had been through, and the focused, confident Detective Sergeant had inspired her. Although quick fixes and riches were one thing, there was no substitute for doing the right thing.

From a purely selfish point of view, she also suspected that this was some sort of test. Perhaps they were trying to see how trustworthy she was, in order that she could be trusted with even bigger stories in future. After all, who knew what went on behind closed doors? A fleeting thought crossed her mind — only for a moment — that they might even be feeding her scraps of false information to try and trace leaks. She knew plenty of colleagues who'd been caught out that way.

When she'd joined the Mildenheath Gazette, Suzanne had had the pleasure of working briefly with Don Norman, a veteran journalist who'd enjoyed a long and fruitful career on the local newspaper and had even had a brief foray into radio and television journalism. He'd told her to always remember what her values and belief systems were before she ever first set foot in a newspaper office. That way, he said, she'd always be true to herself.

It was those words that rung loudly in her ears now as she convinced herself that the urge to take the money and run just wasn't her. It was something that had wormed its way in and instilled itself in her purely by being surrounded by this culture of dirty journalism.

Suzanne wanted to do things differently. She knew that trust and honour went a long way — much further than many other journalists realised or appreciated — and she was certain that she could carve her way with honesty and respect.

It was a classic psychological battle. She recalled seeing an experiment on an episode of *Horizon* one time, in which young children were offered a bag of sweets right that second or the opportunity to wait ten minutes and get two bags of sweets. The overwhelming majority went for instant gratification. The understanding of delayed rewards was something that only came with maturity, and she chuckled at the realisation that many of her colleagues were no more psychologically advanced than the four-year-olds on TV.

One other thing Suzanne Corrigan knew that her colleagues didn't was that tomorrow was going to be one of the biggest days in the history of crime in the UK.

58

8TH NOVEMBER

As with everything in policing, it was all about balance. The knee-jerk reaction would've been to have put the entire town on lockdown, imposed a curfew and had anyone in public arrested on sight. Aside from the impracticalities, that was an approach which would have done more harm than good.

Simply doing nothing and waiting to see what happened wasn't an option either. It certainly wasn't something the family and friends of the fifth dead woman would be too pleased to find out about. A balance had to be achieved, and everyone at Mildenheath CID was satisfied that it had been.

Culverhouse had managed — through the assistance of Chief Constable Hawes — to fend off the flailing claws of Malcolm Pope, who'd been suggested as someone who could come in to aid the investigation. Hawes had put his job on the line to convince the Police and Crime Commissioner that everything was under control. In any other CID department, a string of Detective Superintendents and Chief Superintendents would've been able to step in and restructure the team to suit the investigation, but Culverhouse was grateful for the unconventional and archaic county setup which meant that he — for now — answered directly to the Chief Constable. Should tonight's efforts not result in the killer being caught, that would all end.

All major roads into Mildenheath would have roadblocks and traffic checkpoints in place by eight o'clock that evening. The public would not be forewarned, but simply asked to state who they were and where they were going. Anyone on the watch list which had been generated throughout the investigation would be immediately held for further questioning. Anyone passing through the town would be directed back out and around — for the most part towards the main M1 motorway, on which the Mildenheath exit junction would be shut too.

Officers had been drafted in from a number of neighbouring forces, with riot vans, squad cars and a range of response vehicles being brought in too. All registered PCSOs within a particular radius had been called in as well as mobile CCTV vans having been drafted in to give extra coverage over certain areas of the town. The police presence on the streets of Mildenheath would be unprecedented.

The list of suspects had, by now, been exhausted. A string of interviews had got them next to nowhere, with their only link being to the hairdressing salon. Everyone who worked at the salon had been interviewed to no avail, and Queenie Kinsella had long been discounted as a suspect. In the absence of anything else, the coincidence was undeniable, but any direct link was completely unprovable.

'Does anyone have any questions at all?' Culverhouse asked the assembled CID officers in the incident room, both Wendy and Luke Baxter conspicuous in their absence.

'Not really a question, but a slight nagging concern, guv,'

Debbie Weston said. 'I know we need as many officers on the frontline as we can tonight, but I have this worry that we might be falling into a trap. The killer's proven to be at least one step ahead at all times so far. How do we know this isn't just another deliberate ploy to get us where he wants us? What if he's just trying to distract police resources for some reason?'

'Well it's a bit fucking late to raise that now, isn't it?' Culverhouse barked.

Patrick Sharp, the psychological profiler, stepped forward from behind Culverhouse. 'In fact, I'd think that was unlikely. According to his profile, I'd strongly expect him to follow his MO. It compels him to try and kill a victim who fits his criteria again tonight. He won't deviate from that.'

'Besides which,' Culverhouse added, 'it'll be uniform on the streets. We're going to need to hang around for when something kicks off, so if you fancy playing desk sergeant for the night, the job's all yours.'

'What if that's the whole plan all along, though?' Debbie asked, clearly getting nowhere.

'I'm confident it isn't,' Patrick Sharp replied, smiling.

'You say he won't deviate, but what about the second letter? That was a deviation.'

'All I can do is repeat what I've already said. He got desperate. There are only two outcomes here. Either he succeeds and kills his fifth victim, or we catch him.'

59

Although the station was eerily quiet that night, the officers who remained were far from subdued. There was an odd atmosphere of exterior calm but with a clear and permeating sense of heightened alertness.

Debbie Weston found herself pacing around the incident room, her heart pounding in her ears as she glanced at the clock every few seconds. She kept running through the facts in her head. They knew the fifth victim was likely to be of Welsh or Irish descent, possibly a prostitute, possibly having had a husband die in a tragic accident at a young age. She knew it was unlikely the intended victim would match all of these criteria. Every victim up until now had only matched one or two, which was what had made identifying the fifth victim completely impossible.

She knew she was going to get nowhere. She'd been going over it in her mind for weeks, and she knew she needed to keep a calm and level head. Like the guv said, they were the response team now. They had to wait and entrust the officers on the streets with the intelligence they'd gathered so far.

She hadn't smoked in a long time, but she always kept a sneaky pack of cigarettes in the glove compartment of her dented, faded Vauxhall Cavalier. Without a second thought, she jogged down the stairs and let herself out into the car park.

Debbie flung open the glove compartment and rummaged around inside, her hands running over a selection of receipts and parking tickets. She found the pack of cigarettes. There were still four left. Bingo. She picked up the folded piece of paper which had fallen out during her rummage and was about to put it back in the glove compartment when she saw what was written on it.

It was the home address of Suzanne Corrigan, the journalist from the local paper. She'd given them her home address in case they wanted to contact her out of hours. She'd jotted down her mobile number on a separate piece of paper somewhere, too, but Debbie was buggered if she was going to be able to find that.

Llanedeyrn, 21 Mark Street, Mildenheath.

Debbie chuckled as she saw the address, as she had when Suzanne Corrigan had first handed her the piece of paper. Mark Street wasn't the sort of road where many owners gave their houses names, to say the least. Most didn't even give them a lick of paint, so Debbie had automatically questioned what she had seen as a rather pretentious act. Suzanne had been quick to mention that Llanedeyrn was the area of Cardiff she'd been brought up in, and that it reminded her of home. She'd also mentioned that her parents did a similar thing when they moved over from Belfast, calling their new house in Wales *Castlereagh*.

Debbie's face soon turned from amusement to horrific sudden realisation as she threw the slip of paper and packet of cigarettes into her footwell, jumped into the driver's seat and started the engine.

As she sped off towards the town centre, she fumbled around in her pocket for her mobile. Bugger. She'd left it on her desk. She could even see it sat there in her mind's eye. She decided against turning back. Time was of the essence.

60

Wendy and Luke Baxter had headed north to a village pub not far from county police HQ at Milton House. As the pub was not only fairly rural but also popular with the police, the owners were willing, more often than not, to stay open well beyond their usual hours.

They knew, too, that they were likely to get a call before too long to let them know that they'd either apprehended the killer or found another body, so this was going to be no early night for either of them.

This wasn't the way Wendy wanted to spend her evening, but she'd been told by Culverhouse that she needed to clear the air with Luke. They'd been sat in near silence for a good few minutes, neither of them really knowing what to say to each other.

'That Desmond Jordan's up for the chop,' Baxter said, taking a sip of his pint. 'CPS are going to charge him over the assault in the pub, apparently.'

'Good,' Wendy replied. 'He's a slimy bastard. Deserves

everything he gets coming to him.' Jordan's infidelities would undoubtedly prove to be the unraveling of his marriage, not to mention his career, but it had at least had the unintended consequence of clearing him of multiple murders.

The silence fell over Wendy and Luke once again, neither of them particularly wanting to be here or being especially interested in making small talk.

'What's the point in this?' Wendy finally said. 'I'm never going to like you and you're never going to like me. Can we just leave it at that?'

'Always the optimist, aren't you?' Luke replied. 'Look, I know you've been through a lot of shit but why let the job suffer? I'm not saying we need to be best mates, but I think we can at least be civil.'

Wendy was stunned into silence. It certainly wasn't like Luke Baxter to be the voice of reason and extend an olive branch. 'Someone spiked your drink or something?'

Luke laughed. 'The job stresses you out at times. I get it. It does with me, too. It does with all of us. And yeah, we've got different ways of doing things. But so what? You get on alright with the guv. He's not that much different from me.'

'It's not the same,' Wendy replied. 'You're a climber. He's spent years doing the hard graft. You were parachuted in and fast-tracked because you spend all your time licking his arse.'

'Is that really what you think?' Luke said, leaning forward. 'Let me tell you something. I always wanted to be a copper. Ever since I was young. You want to know why I never talk about my family life? When I was five, my parents were coming home from a weekend away. I'd been staying with my dad's sister. They were driving back home when a car sideswiped them at a set of traffic lights. The people in the other car were being chased by the police. My mum and dad died instantly. My aunt and uncle took me in and brought me up, but all I ever wanted was to join the police and try and put things right. Try to make sure those mistakes didn't happen to other people. But I could never get in. So yeah, I went to uni and they put me through the fast-track programme. You know yourself how little you can actually do on the streets. You're always being shat on from up high, paperwork, bureaucratic procedure. There's fuck all you can do as a bobby to put anything right. So yeah, I'm trying to get as far up the ladder as I can. Not to feather my own nest, but to make a difference.'

Wendy swallowed and looked down at her drink. 'I'm sorry, Luke. I didn't know.'

'No. No-one does. It's not something I go broadcasting. But at the same time I don't expect people to just make their own judgements based on nothing.'

'It must be hard,' Wendy said, not knowing what else to say.

'Yeah. Course. But you just have to wear this disguise, don't you? Pretend you're a big brave boy and that you don't give a shit about anything. Because, inside, I'm still that scared little five-year-old boy. That was the day everything stopped.'

'You don't have to wear a disguise, Luke. The world's moved on. You don't lose points for being sensitive and emotional any more. Besides, there are better disguises than the one you've been putting on since you've been working here.'

Luke laughed. 'I'll just nip down the fancy dress shop and grab myself a Batman outfit then, shall I? Wear that to work instead.'

'More like Pratman,' Wendy joked, feeling the tension and

atmosphere lift as they shared a laugh for the first time since they'd met. No sooner had she registered her enjoyment of this feeling, she was hit like a bolt from the blue. 'Fuck. Fancy dress shop.'

'What?' Luke said, taking a mouthful of beer.

'Fancy dress shop! There's one next door to Terri Kinsella's salon, isn't there?'

'Uh, sort of. Not fancy dress, though. I think it does more theatrical costume hire. Proper professional stuff. I don't think they'd have a Batman outfit.'

Wendy stood suddenly. 'Don't you remember? Queenie Kinsella said her son ran the shop next door. The costume hire shop! That's how it was done! Old Queenie went blabbing to her son about the lives of her customers, and meanwhile Paul's compiling his dossier of Mildenheath's women, waiting for his perfect five!' She grabbed her mobile phone from her pocket, walked quickly to leave the pub and phoned Frank Vine.

'Frank? It's Wendy,' she said as she noticed Luke follow her out, carrying both coats. 'Listen, can you check an address for me please? It's for a Paul Kinsella. Owns the costume hire shop on Eastfield Road. Cheers.'

'Shit, I've just had a thought,' Luke said, while Wendy waited for Frank to check the address. 'If he runs a costume hire shop—'

'Yes, he'd have a policeman's uniform,' Wendy said, cutting him off. 'That's how he gets people's trust and managed to avoid suspicion on the night Emma and Marla were killed.' She spun on her feet as Frank Vine's voice came back on the phone. 'Seriously? Fuck. Fuck fuck fuck! We're about twenty minutes away, but I'll call her now.'

'What is it?' Luke asked, jogging to keep up with Wendy, who was now sprinting across the car park to her car.

'Paul Kinsella's address. 19 Mark Street. He lives next door to Suzanne Corrigan.'

Suzanne had allowed herself one small glass of red wine. Although she knew she'd probably have to dash out at some point within the next few hours, she needed to steady her nerves.

She leant back on her sofa and closed her eyes for a few moments, letting the alcohol work its magic as she tried to calm her brain and let the noise quieten down. Just as she was about to drift off to sleep, the ringing of the doorbell jolted her awake and back to reality.

She looked at her watch. Almost midnight. Far later than most reasonable people would think about ringing someone's doorbell, but that was Mildenheath for you. She walked to the front door, her slippers scuffing against the laminate flooring as she shuffled her way.

Taking off the chain and turning the key, she glanced through the eyehole before opening the door and smiling pleasantly.

'Oh, it's you.'

'Fuck, there's still no answer,' Luke said as Wendy sped down the dual carriageway touching one hundred miles an hour. They'd shave a good amount of time off the journey, but it'd still be a good twenty to twenty-five minutes before they'd reach Suzanne Corrigan's house.

'Don't worry. Uniform will be on their way. They'll be there before us. We'd just better hope they make it in time.'

'I've had a thought,' Luke said, putting the phone in his lap. What if Paul Kinsella's out there in uniform? I mean, we don't even know what he looks like. What if he's milling around with the specials and guys from other forces?'

'I don't think he'll risk that,' Wendy replied, speeding past a dodgy-looking white van that she'd be tempted to pull over in any other circumstance. 'They'd be able to tell, surely.'

'Not necessarily. A fancy dress costume, yes, but a proper replica uniform for theatre or film hire? The whole point is they're meant to look real.'

Wendy took a couple of moments to compose her thoughts. 'Right. Call Culverhouse. Ask him — no, tell him — not to send uniform in. If he asks why, tell him... Tell him to trust me.'

Baxter tried to stifle a laugh as he found Culverhouse's name in his phone's contacts list. 'Do you really think he's going to go with that?'

'I don't know, but it's got to be worth trying. Tell him we're ten minutes away. At the most.'

Debbie Weston parked her Cavalier up outside number 21 Mark Street. It looked pleasant enough, but she was in no position to admire the architecture, noticing the bright red front door was slightly ajar.

As she got closer, she could hear a mobile phone ringing inside. It stopped, then started again. She pushed open the door and called inside.

'Hello?'

No answer. She walked in and found herself immediately in Suzanne Corrigan's living room. The only sign of life was a half-drunk glass of wine on the nest of tables next to the sofa.

'Hello?' she called again.

Still nothing.

She peered up the stairs, but was met with darkness. Putting her foot on the first step, she slowly made her way up, calling out as she went.

As she reached the top of the stairs, she could hear a murmur from what seemed like the back bedroom.

She walked up to the door and put her ear up against it, listening. That murmuring again.

Debbie put her hand on the doorknob and slowly turned it, hearing it creak and squeal slightly as it turned. With a click, the door opened and Debbie peered inside to find Suzanne Corrigan's eyes glistening in the moonlight, silver tape plastered over her mouth as she murmured and whimpered, tied to the bed, her eyes pleading desperately.

She took a step towards Suzanne and reached out to loosen her bonds, but was stopped dead in her tracks by the sudden sound of a man's voice.

'Oh, I wouldn't do that if I was you.'

Fortunately for Culverhouse, he'd managed to stop the uniformed officers reaching Suzanne Corrigan's house just in time. They were barely fifty yards from the turning into her street, but he'd managed to hold them off. He still wasn't sure why he'd done it, but he knew that a hunch from Wendy was often right. Having glanced at his watch, he knew they probably had a couple of hours before the Ripper would kill again, so decided to trust Wendy's judgement.

Despite that, he'd called Baxter straight back, demanding an immediate explanation. Luke told him everything about the costume hire shop and Wendy's theory that Paul Kinsella could be disguising himself as a uniformed police officer. The only way they could make sure he couldn't get near Suzanne Corrigan — assuming he wasn't already there or in his house next door — was to go in themselves.

He personally cleared Wendy and Luke to go to Suzanne's house in their unmarked vehicle, knowing that he'd have to stay where he was and make a very interesting call to the Chief Constable.

• • •

'Who are you?' Debbie asked, backing into the room as the man walked towards her, staring down the barrel of the pistol. He was dressed in a police uniform, but Debbie knew instinctively that this man had never been a police officer in his life.

'Who am I, or what's my name?' the man replied, in a calm voice, smiling.

'Both.'

'My name's Paul. And I think you know who I am. Who are you?'

Debbie's calves hit the edge of the bed and she could step back no further. 'My name's Debbie. Put the gun down and we can talk.'

'Are you a copper?' he asked, his eyebrows raised and head cocked slightly to the side.

'They'll be surrounding the house as we speak. They've got armed units trained on the house,' Debbie lied.

Paul Kinsella laughed a deep, guttural belly laugh. 'Don't be stupid. If that was the case, they wouldn't have sent you in. You're alone. I know you are.'

Debbie tried to stop the fear showing in her eyes, but it wasn't easy.

The flash of light seared through the window only for a second or two as the noise of the police helicopter became a deafening roar. It was brief, but it was enough for Paul to glance towards the window, allowing Debbie to knock the gun out of his hand and slam the heel of her hand up into his nose.

As the gun skidded across the laminate floor, Debbie scrambled to undo Suzanne's bonds, her hands shaking uncontrollably as she did so.

She glanced over at Paul. He seemed to be unconscious. For now.

Finally, the ties came loose and Suzanne was on her feet, clambering across the room and yanking the door open. She was already halfway down the stairs when Debbie decided to forget trying to find the gun and to follow her instead.

Just as she reached the bedroom doorway, she felt the firm grip of two hands around her right ankle as the ground rushed up to meet her.

Wendy's car squealed round the corner into Mark Street, and she immediately saw the familiar sight of Debbie Weston's battered old Cavalier parked right outside Suzanne Corrigan's house.

'Fuck! What's Debbie doing here?' she yelled, yanking the handbrake and flinging open her door.

'Shit, Wendy, look,' Luke said, pointing at Suzanne's front door. 'I don't like the look of that.'

'Get onto the DCI. Tell him what's going on,' Wendy said, making for the house.

'No! Like hell am I letting you go in there. You call him. And stay *outside* the house. I need you to keep an eye out.'

Before Wendy could argue, Luke had skipped up the front step and was in the house.

The light was on downstairs, which was odd as it seemed like no-one was in the house. The half-drunk glass of wine said otherwise, though.

Luke was careful to keep quiet, treading gently as he stalked through the house, careful not to make himself heard.

As he reached the top of the stairs, he glanced into the spare bedroom and saw Debbie Weston sitting on the bed, with a man in a police uniform knelt behind her, his arm around her neck with a gun pressed to her temple.

'Your friend here just did something very silly,' the man said, through gritted teeth. 'I have a plan and I need to stick to it. I don't get very happy when people change my plans for me.'

'Put the gun down,' Luke said, holding one hand out at arm's length, trying to placate the man. 'What do you want?'

'I want my number five back. I want my Mary Jane.'

'Suzanne? You can't. She's gone,' Luke said, not knowing where Suzanne was.

'What a shame. Because I'm going to get my number five, whichever way,' the man replied, pressing the gun harder against Debbie's head. 'And if it's not going to be the one I wanted, it's going to be your friend here.'

Culverhouse was on his way to Mark Street as quickly as he could, driving at fifty miles an hour down Mildenheath High Street whilst talking to Wendy on his mobile. Not something he would have condoned at any other time, but this was different.

'Uniform just radioed in to say that Suzanne Corrigan got away,' he said. 'She's with them now, by the old grammar school. What's going on down there?'

'I don't know. Luke's gone inside, but I've not heard anything yet,' Wendy replied.

'He's done what? The fucking idiot. Whatever you do, don't follow him. I'll be there in two minutes.'

. . .

'Why don't you take me instead?' Luke said, his voice quivering as he spoke. 'Leave Debbie alone. She's not done anything.'

'She lost me my number five!' Paul yelled, his eyes mad and bloodshot.

'It's over. Why put yourself through even more? Why take more lives? You're young. If you give yourself up now, you might get back out again. If you kill a copper, you'll never get out. Not these days.'

'You're assuming they're going to catch me,' Paul said quietly and calmly.

'They will. Believe me, they will. They already have.'

Paul snorted and guffawed as Luke watched the snot drip from his nose. 'If that was the case, I'd be in the back of your car in handcuffs, not sitting here watching you snivel as I hold your friend's life in my hands.'

'Listen, you don't need to do this,' Luke said, holding his hands out. 'Just let her go. It's over now.'

Before Paul could respond, the figure of Jack Culverhouse bundled in through the bedroom door. 'Right, pack it in, knobhead.'

Startled, Luke tried to speak. 'Guv, I—'

'Save it, Baxter. I know a real gun when I see one. What's that, Paul? Another little toy from your shop? What is it, theatrical replica? Starting pistol?'

Paul broke into a smile, showing his glistening white teeth as he loosened his grip on Debbie's neck and turned to point the gun at Culverhouse. 'Well, why don't we find out?'

Without a moment's hesitation, seeing Paul's finger begin to squeeze the trigger, Luke threw himself towards Culverhouse, pulling him to the floor as the deafening shot rang out, the sound echoing and reverberating around the room.

Debbie took her chance. She braced her leg against the wall and shoulder-barged Paul as hard as she could, knocking him off balance.

As she pulled away and turned to aim a kick at his head, she noticed he had already recovered and was cowering in the corner, pointing the gun at her once again.

Before he could speak, the sound of the armed response officers thundering up the stairs momentarily stunned Paul.

'Bit late, lads,' he said, cocking the gun. 'I'm afraid the damage is done.'

With a swift movement, he placed the barrel of the gun in his mouth and pulled the trigger.

'Suspect down!' the first armed officer yelled into his radio. 'I repeat, suspect down!'

Wendy rushed into the room and went straight to Debbie, checking she was alright and comforting her immediately.

Culverhouse, however, was less than happy. 'Will you fucking get off me, you great lump?' he barked in Luke's ear from his face-down position on the floor, not seeing the deep crimson liquid that was soaking into his shirt.

Wendy took a moment to process what was happening as she looked over at her fellow officers. 'Luke? Luke, can you hear me?'

'Fucking get him off me!' Culverhouse yelled, wriggling like a beached whale.

From Luke, there was no response.

'Fuck. Luke? Luke, can you hear me?' Wendy shouted into his face, pressing her two fingers into the side of his neck to check for a pulse. She felt the panic rise up in her chest. 'Guv, call an ambulance. Now.'

64

Mildenheath Hospital didn't hold happy memories for Wendy. Whenever she'd visited on work it had inevitably been depressing, as hospitals and police work tended to be. Even her private visits had been ones to want to forget, from her parents' deaths to her brother's hospitalisation after a drug overdose. The solemn mood that accompanied her, Culverhouse and Debbie Weston this time, though, was something she'd never felt before.

Being a police officer was a job that carried a certain amount of risk. All officers knew that. But none actually expected to be shot in the line of duty. Especially not a CID officer, who was generally kept away from the front line.

There had been incidents in the past, of course, but nothing quite like this. Wendy herself had been hit by a car whilst chasing a suspect on foot not long ago, and as a result had suffered a miscarriage. That had been bad enough, but it had been a strange sort of private pain. The death of a person whom only she had ever known. Hearing the frantic sounds of the medical team battling to keep Luke Baxter alive was something very different. It was the desperate anguish of the life of a colleague — a friend — hanging in the balance. The unspoken truth was also that it could have just as easily been any one of them.

Luke's aunt, Shirley, was inconsolable, looking like a lost puppy as she kept glancing up at the door to the intensive care unit, desperate to be allowed in but told by the doctors and surgeons to stay outside and try and keep calm. Her other nephew, Luke's older brother, Sam, was doing his best to console her.

For Wendy, she wished desperately she could say something to them. She'd been in that position herself, when she'd found out what had happened to her dad. It wasn't something she wished on anybody and she felt every bit of Shirley and Sam's pain.

Just as she was considering trying to say something to them — some words which could go some way towards reassuring or comforting them — the door to the intensive care unit opened and a middle-aged female doctor came out and sat down with Shirley and Sam.

From where Wendy was sitting, she couldn't hear the words the doctor said, but the reaction from Luke's aunt said everything. As she saw Shirley's world fall apart in fits of hysterical sobbing, Wendy knew exactly what had been said.

The mood in the major incident room was far more sombre than it otherwise would've been. Yes, they'd managed to avoid the fifth murder, but it had come at a huge cost. Not only had they failed to get their man alive, but the death of Luke Baxter had had an enormous impact on everyone who worked at Mildenheath CID.

It was rare that any officer was lost on operational duty, and it was even less likely for a CID officer. For Jack Culverhouse and Debbie Weston, the outcome was particularly bittersweet. As far as they were concerned, Luke Baxter had died a hero. He'd put himself in harm's way to save Debbie and had given his life in protecting Culverhouse.

Even Wendy had to admit that she'd come to respect Luke somewhat after they'd cleared the air earlier that night. She was thankful that they'd been able to do that.

The local and national news channels were all running the story about how a brave police officer had been killed in the line of duty whilst saving the life of a serial killer's fifth intended victim. Suzanne Corrigan's name was, once again, all over the papers but this time it wasn't as part of the byline. There were the predictable calls from some areas of the media for the police to explain why the public at large weren't made aware of the threat that had existed, but that wasn't something the Chief Constable felt obliged to answer at that moment in time.

The police were still trying to come to terms with why Paul Kinsella had done what he'd done, as well as how. Finding his victims had been fairly straightforward — his mother's inability to keep anything to herself had helped with that. His home was being searched at that moment in time, and the officers had already found notebooks full of plans and names — many of them scribbled out. The lucky ones. From what they could ascertain at this early stage, it seemed that one of his female friends had been sexually assaulted a few years earlier, and the police had failed to charge the suspect. Judging by the scribblings in his notebooks, his mind was far from stable and he seemed to consider it perfectly justified to take innocent lives in order to prove his hypothesis that the modern day police force were no better than Victorian plods.

The whole episode had resulted in a very strange atmosphere around Mildenheath CID. It wasn't just the absence of Luke Baxter that was odd, but the presence of Martin Cummings, the Police and Crime Commissioner, who'd come to address the team. He was, unsurprisingly, viewed with suspicion. After the recent rumours about merging Mildenheath CID at county HQ to try and cut costs, Cummings was far less popular than he usually was — which wasn't very popular at all. Culverhouse certainly wouldn't have put it past him to come and announce the move on a morning like this. As far as he was concerned, the man's tactlessness knew no bounds. And coming from Jack Culverhouse, that was quite something.

'Firstly, I just wanted to both congratulate you on your success and commiserate you on your loss,' Cummings said, his hands clasped in front of him. 'I understand Luke was a very bright and talented young officer with a strong future ahead of him. He put all that at risk in order to protect his fellow officers. I'll be speaking with the Chief Constable in due course to see how we can honour his memory and ensure that his sacrifice is not forgotten.'

Charles Hawes nodded as Cummings continued.

'Now, I know there's been a lot of talk about the proposed merger of Mildenheath CID into Milton Hall. I thought it might brighten your spirits slightly if I were to let you know that the plan is currently on hold.'

'Sorry, sir,' Culverhouse said, interrupting. 'By on hold, do you mean it's off?'

Cummings looked slightly uncomfortable. 'It seems so, yes. But I must stress that this was due to logistical matters. It is in no way a reflection on feedback from officers or any recent cases.'

There were a few sniggers and knowing looks exchanged. They knew Cummings would never have been able to justify scrapping the CID setup — not after this.

'Now, I just wanted you all to know how proud I am of you. If there's anything else I can do, please do let me know.'

'Actually, there is one other thing,' Culverhouse said, raising his hand.

'Yes?'

'Tell Malcolm Pope I send my regards.'

GET MORE OF MY BOOKS FREE!

Thank you for reading *Jack Be Nimble*. I hope it was as much fun for you as it was for me writing it.

To say thank you, I'd like to give you some of my books and short stories for FREE. Read on to get yours...

If you enjoyed the book, please do leave a review on Amazon. Reviews mean an awful lot to writers and they help us to find new readers more than almost anything else. It would be very much appreciated.

I love hearing from my readers, too, so please do feel free to get in touch with me. You can contact me via my website, on Twitter @adamcroft and you can 'like' my Facebook page at http://www.facebook.com/adamcroftbooks.

Last of all, but certainly not least, I'd like to let you know that members of my VIP club have access to FREE, exclusive books and short stories which aren't available anywhere else. There's a whole lot more, too, so please join the club (for free!) at adamcroft.net/VIP-club

For more information, visit my website: adamcroft.net

Who hunts the hunters?

When a man is found dead, mutilated in his house, DS Wendy Knight and DCI Jack Culverhouse soon realise that Jeff Brelsford was killed for one reason: he was a paedophile.

As Wendy does her job and tries to find the killer, Culverhouse is less keen. As far as he's concerned, this is justice.

With Culverhouse's attitude and stubbornness leaving him on the sidelines, Wendy delves deeper into the dark and murky world of Jeff Brelsford, and what she discovers is enough to shock her to her core.

Could it be that the killer was someone very close to home... a police officer?

Turn the page to read the first chapter...

ROUGH JUSTICE
CHAPTER 1

Jeff Brelsford poured the last dregs of the coffee from the jug and switched off the hot-plate. The dark liquid steamed from his mug as the bitter aroma assaulted his nostrils.

It was late for coffee, but Jeff wasn't on Greenwich Mean Time with the rest of Mildenheath; he was running on Pacific Time. His contacts on the California coast would just be finishing their late breakfast or lunch and logging on to the forum.

The adrenaline surged in Jeff's chest every time he sat down at his laptop, opened TorBrowser and waited for the status bar to tell him the connection to the Tor network had been made and that he was completely protected and cloaked in anonymity.

The Dark Web was where Jeff had been spending most of his time recently. It was a safe haven where he was able to find like-minded people who truly understood how it felt to be like him. He didn't think he was a bad man. He hadn't harmed anyone. Not directly, anyway.

It was a confusing place to be, inside a mind conflicted

between a burning desire and a sense of injustice at what he saw to be a lack of understanding, stacked up against the knowledge that the rest of the world saw his predilections as vile and despicable. Deep down, he knew they were right. Underneath it all he knew his desires, although under control for now, could easily become dangerous.

He also knew he couldn't let that happen. He'd already been satisfying his desires to a degree that worried him, even though he was under the relative anonymity of the Dark Web.

By its very nature, the Dark Web was almost completely anonymous. An area of the internet based on hidden protocols, invisible to search engines and general users, the Dark Web was accessible only using the TorBrowser software. It had become home to enormous online drug markets, with websites such as Silk Road openly and brazenly offering illicit narcotics for sale, safe in the knowledge that the very structure of the Dark Web made it very difficult for anyone to find out who ran the sites or who their customers were.

The common currency of the Dark Web, Bitcoin, allowed users to exchange money under the radar without linking it to their bank account or personal identity. In short, anything could be bought on the Dark Web, whether it be guns, fraudulently obtained credit card details or even hired assassins. Compared to that, Jeff had managed to convince himself that looking at photographs of young girls was relatively innocuous.

The forum had been set up a few months previously, unlisted on any Dark Web directories in order to ensure that only those who knew about it and had been personally invited would be able to access it. Jeff had been invited by a member of another forum, Deepest Desires, of which he'd been a member for a couple of years. Being invited to be part of the new, unnamed, forum had left Jeff feeling like the privileged new member of a secret club, heightening the surge of adrenaline he got every time he accessed it.

As Jeff saw it, it was far better that he and the other members of the forum got their kicks sharing pictures and titillating comments than actually going out and acting on their desires. That had got him into trouble before, and he couldn't go making that mistake again.

He gulped down two mouthfuls of the bitter coffee and licked his lips, catching the rogue droplets before they splashed onto the desk in front of him.

The laptop lid was barely open when the doorbell rang, the harsh, shrill ringing catching him unawares and giving him a sudden start. He wasn't expecting visitors. He reasoned it was probably someone collecting for charity or trying to sell double-glazing, knocking on doors in the evening assuming that they'd be able to catch people at home.

He unlatched the door and pulled it open. The man who stood on the other side of the door was certainly not who he'd expected.

'Jeff Brelsford?' the man said, his hands pushed into the trouser pockets of his dark suit as he cocked his head sideways.

'Yeah, why?' Jeff replied, sensing that something wasn't quite right.

'I'm Detective Inspector Richard Thomson. Can I come in?'

Jeff faltered for a moment. Had he somehow dropped a bollock on the Dark Web and managed to allow the police to track him down? No, it wasn't possible.

Then again, it could be to do with the double-yellows he'd parked on a couple of weeks back. It had only been for a couple of minutes and he hadn't been given a ticket. Or had he? Had it

blown off the windscreen and been logged on a system somewhere that he'd ignored it? No, they wouldn't get CID involved
with something like that.

'Uh, have you got any ID?' Jeff asked, stalling for time.

'Certainly,' the man replied, taking his hands out of his
trouser pockets and going to his inside jacket pocket.

Before Jeff could realise what the black and yellow unit in
the man's hand was, his entire body went rigid and he lost all
motor skills as twelve-hundred volts seared through his testicles.

Want to read on?

**Visit adamcroft.net/book/rough-justice/ to grab
your copy.**

ACKNOWLEDGMENTS

As always, a number of people are responsible for making this book what is. So blame them, not me.

My special thanks go to:

PC Matthew Taylor and the rest of the First Response team at Bedfordshire Police for letting me shadow him for the day and see the fantastic job the police do in responding to incidents.

My wife and mum for being the first people to read my early drafts and fix my most laughable errors before they ever see the light of day.

My fantastic Advanced Readers Club, who read the book before anyone else and give their feedback on plots, characters and the other laughable errors. They are Gary Alce, Lisa Gall, Cynthia Philo and Laura Smith. In my eyes, they're all gods.

Thanks also to everyone else not thanked by name, but who I should be thanking. I appear to have mislaid my list of people to thank, and I'm on a deadline here, dontchaknow. If you were expecting to be thanked on this page and haven't been, please don't take it personally — I've either lost the list or one of my cats has eaten it.

I hope you enjoy the book, and I'd very much welcome any feedback you have.

Adam Croft

CPSIA information can be obtained
at www.ICGtesting.com
Printed in the USA
LVHW040540090721
692259LV00007B/469